THE HOUSE

COME FIND YOUR FANTASY

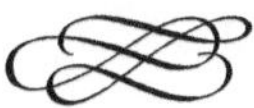

CASSIE ALEXANDER

CASKARA PRESS

The House

Copyright © 2021 by Cassie Alexander. All rights reserved.

No part of this publication may be reproduced, distributed, or transmitted in any form or by any means, including photocopying, recording, or other electronic or mechanical methods, without the prior written permission of the publisher, except in the case of brief quotations embodied in critical reviews and certain other noncommercial uses permitted by copyright law. For permission requests, email cassandraassistant@gmail.com.

www.cassiealexander.com

Publisher's Note: This is a work of fiction. Names, characters, places, and incidents are a product of the author's imagination. Locales and public names are sometimes used for atmospheric purposes. Any resemblance to actual people, living or dead, or to businesses, companies, events, institutions, or locales is completely coincidental.

❀ Created with Vellum

If you'd like to join Cassie's mailing list, click here or go to https://www.cassiealexander.com/newsletter – for sneak peeks, book news, playlists, and cat photos!

ACKNOWLEDGEMENTS

Generous thanks to Gemma Depolo for her fabulous idea.

*Y*ou are a modern woman recently on the outside of a rough marriage after a rougher divorce.

While immersing yourself in the business of putting your radically different life back together, you receive a small package in the mail. Convinced that it belongs to your rental's prior tenant and dismayed that they left no forwarding address, you leave it on your kitchen table for three days with good intentions to contact the landlord – after you finish unpacking and forwarding all of your own bills.

It is not until the fourth night that you realize that it is indeed addressed to you.

YOU PICK the package up and take it into your living room. There's something inside that moves when you shake it but it doesn't feel fragile. Alone on your couch, you cut through the tape sealing the box and open it up – upside down. A key falls to the floor at your feet, and when you flip the lid of the box, you notice a note on fine stationary pressed inside.

The key is strung on a ribbon. It is silver, ornate, and delicate and looks like it was meant for a very fine jewelry box. You question just what it does open – and why someone would be sending it to you. You pick the key up and set it on the coffee table you just picked up at a thrift store earlier in the evening.

The note, like the package, is addressed to you by name. It's on the type of paper that you only see on movies, linen with frayed edges so thick it's almost fabric, which seems to give the words written on it greater weight.

The Master of the House has chosen you.

This key opens the House and all the doors inside. You will be in complete control of all your experiences in the House – and what you find there will exceed the heights of your imagination.

The opportunity of a lifetime awaits you -- all you need to do is bring me back my key.

M

IN THE BOTTOM of the box are two airline tickets. One to the House, and one back. The flight leaves tomorrow.

Will you take it? If so, turn to page 3.

If not, turn to page 247.

*I*t's hard not to think you've made a crazy choice. But you haven't gotten a job yet, and you tell yourself that [redacted] is a perfectly nice place to go. Perhaps you'll just fly up there and wander around. Maybe you won't even leave the airport. At least it's not your hometown anymore, where every corner seems overburdened with memories.

Which is why even though you doubt yourself, you're at the airport at 2 PM in a nice shirt and skirt the next day.

YOUR TICKETS ARE for first class, which you've never flown before. The flight attendants are pleasant and serve you lobster and champagne. The flight alone has earned out your curiosity -- you'll have plenty to talk about now with new friends, once you make them.

It's only when the plane begins to circle to land that you get nervous. You have no intentions of actually visiting the House. This trip has just been some sort of crazy lark, probably a mix-up due to your somewhat common name.

You're still considering staying on the plane and taking the return flight back when the flight attendant comes by and tells you that your driving service has called to inform you that your driver has arrived downstairs.

You've never had a driver take you anywhere that wasn't on a bus. Key in one hand, and return ticket in the other, you take the stairs off of the plane.

PAST BAGGAGE CLAIM there is a beautiful woman dressed in a tailored black suit holding a sign with your last name. You walk past her to see if she recognizes you. She does not – not until you return and come up to her, point at the sign and say, "That's me."

"Do you have the key?" she asks, bright red lips parting with every word.

You hold it up. You've wrapped the ribbon around your wrist and made a bracelet of it. At the sight of the key she smiles generously.

"Please, let me take you to your car."

She takes you to the curb and instructs you to wait for her to return. You stand, nervously clutching the other plane ticket, as other passengers ebb and flow around you like a tide. It is not too late for you to turn around and go, not even when she pulls an expensive black car up, gets out, and holds open your door.

Do you get into the car? If so turn to page 5.

Do you go back into the terminal? If so, go to page 248.

ou slide into the car. The upholstery curves to cradle you like it was sewn specially for the shape of your body, and the seatbelt glides into place with a well-engineered click. The car drives out of the airport and through [redacted] and then soon the city is left behind.

The road undulates over rolling hills like a hand tracing down a woman's side. Driveways peel away at intervals, leading through elaborate gates to the homes hidden behind them. These become more infrequent and the road itself more narrow, until you realize that you are now on a driveway of your own. It makes several broad swoops, through groves of trees and well-manicured lawns, until with a final turn the House appears on the horizon.

It is not really a house – it is a House, with a capital 'H'. It is more like a mansion and then some, the kind of place you only see on TV, that's been changed by economic circumstances into a museum, or a wedding venue, although you would have to invite half of the phone book not to look tiny on its palatial lawn.

Two wings stretch out on either side of the wide driveway, like arms welcoming you to opulence and luxury. In front of you, the center of the house has long white columns at least three stories tall.

The car stops in the precise center, and your driver hops out and walks around to open your door. You look out but then you hesitate. She gives you an encouraging smile.

Do you step out of the car? If so, turn to page 6.

If you stay in the car, go to 249.

She closes the car door behind you once you've exited, then returns to the driver's side and leaves at a leisurely pace, leaving you there in front of the House. It is evening now, and soon the sun will soon set behind you, but right now it reflects off of the House's many windows, giving the House a welcoming glow. You swallow nervously, and then walk up the short path that leads from the driveway and the wide stairs that culminate at the House's front door.

The double-doors are twice as tall as you are and covered in ornate carvings of climbing roses and vines with thorns. Above the door is a phrase carved onto a ribbon of stone:

All is forgiven, all is forgotten.

THE KEY at your wrist is too small for this door, and indeed, you don't even see a lock, so you try to push the left one open. To your surprise, it gives.

You enter into a grand hall with staircases descending on either side. The floor is marble, now lit up with evening's light, and the ceiling is painted with playful maidens, satyrs, and cherubs. Statues of mythological men and women are positioned at intervals along the wall with graceful alabaster limbs, shyly leaning down to pick up clothing as though you've caught them exiting a pool.

You walk out to the middle and stand in awe, looking around the room, when you hear footsteps begin to descend. Turning, you see a man walking down the leftmost stair. He breaks into a smile. There is no confusion with him, he knows who you are, and why you are there.

"You've arrived."

You swallow and nod. "Who are you?"

"The butler." He reaches the landing and then walks over to you, stopping a few feet away. He's elegantly dressed, dark hair, dark eyes, sharp features to match his suit. The only thing that seems to imply his station are the black gloves that cover both his hands. "Do you have the key?" he asks, and you hold it up again. "Good. It is my duty to make sure that you understand the rules."

"Rules? Is this a game – or a test?"

He smiles knowingly and parts his hands. "It is whatever you make of it. Everything is up you to."

"And the master of the house? Where is he?"

"I have no doubt you'll meet him in time." He gestures for you to follow him, and, not sure where else to go, you do.

"The key opens all of the doors in the house, except for the front ones, which are always unlocked." He begins to mount the stairs and you follow, holding onto the gilded railings with your bare hands. "You need not fear losing the key, no one here wants to take it from you – in fact, you can take it with you when you leave, as a memento."

You reach the top of the stairs right after he does. The gilded railings continue, making a hallway along one side of the wall. Huge renaissance paintings alternate with colored doorways. The butler turns to watch your face as he continues speaking.

"You will have from sundown to sunup to do with the House and all of its servants as you will."

"What do you mean?" you say, startled.

"I mean that there will be no consequences from tonight, and no record of what you do here, except for what you take home in your own mind." His lips lift in a subtle smile. "The House is here to serve you, and I am here to serve the House. It is three minutes until sundown. Would you like for me to show you your first doors?"

You swing the key out into your hand. It has a comforting weight to it, like a particularly heavy charm. It has been a long time since you've worn jewelry. You look at the butler, and you nod.

"Some doors you may listen at first, others are purposefully kept as surprises. But remember you may exit any room at any time, the House's servants will not keep you."

He walks over to three doors spaced evenly out. One is white, one is purple, and one is gray. They all seem to pick up and blend with the colors of the paintings beside them.

The butler glances over your shoulder at the distant windows of the front hall. "The sun is down. You are the mistress of the house now, until dawn." He bows deeply. "Please listen, choose, and enjoy."

You step forward and put your ear to the white door. There is the sound of a bath being drawn. If you would like to take a bath, turn to page 9.

You step forward and put your ear to the purple door. There are two men having a conversation inside. If you would like to join them, go to page 193.

You step forward and put your ear to the gray door. Inside are no voices, but there is the hissing sound of rope sliding over rope. If you would like to enter, go to page 54.

The sound of a tub being drawn is familiar, and it calls to you right now. You open the white door and go in.

You would have assumed you'd never see anything as ornate as the grand hall again in your life, but no, it is even more elaborate in here. Every surface is covered in white marble and what isn't marble is gold, and you get the feeling that the gold is real. The room is dominated by a tub that looks like a giant's teacup, and steam is rising from the surface. You wonder who began to draw it and where they went, but they're not here right now, there's nowhere for them to hide.

You walk past a low table with carved feet, piled high with white towels to the tub's side. There is another table closer yet, set with bath salts of different colors in marble bowls beside bathing implements, sponges, soaps, and wash cloths. You take a handful of the purple salts and throw it into the tub and the scent of lavender wafts up. Without thinking about how crazy this could be, you shrug out of your top and bra and pull off your skirt and underwear toss them to the side and sink in. The only thing you're wearing is the bracelet with the key and you feel it thunk against the bottom of the tub.

The water is just the right temperature, hot enough to penetrate your muscles and warm your bones, and the scent is divine. You let out a sigh as the water envelopes you completely up to your neck, then you hold your breath and dip in, until all of you is covered. You stay under, thinking that even if you just stay in here for the whole night, your time will have been well spent.

When you resurface you realize you're not alone. There's a woman as light-skinned as the statues outside, with short tousled orange-red hair, wearing only a bathrobe.

"Who're you?" you ask. You don't feel naked, even though you are, you feel majestic as though this were really your own tub.

"I'm here to help you bathe, if you'd like."

To send her away, turn to page 11.

To invite her in, go to page 14.

"That's all right." You're not ashamed, but you don't need help bathing.

She smiles as though this were expected, although her shoulders slump in disappointment. "Okay. If you'd like though, you can always call me back." She leaves through a door that matches the marble tile in the back of the room.

How odd. Do extraordinarily rich people need help bathing? Or do they just swim around in swimming-pool-sized-tubs? The warm water feels like a second skin. You stroke your hands up your thighs, across your stomach, and cup your own breasts, rubbing your thumb over your nipples. You're all alone in here. Why not have a little fun?

You reach through your legs and pull the gold cord of the drain. It slides open and the water begins draining. You watch it, feeling it lap lower and lower on your body, and start to quiver in anticipation. When there are only a few inches left, you reach up, and turn the faucet on.

The expensive faucet sends the water out in a sheer wall. It isn't hard to position your hips beneath this so that it falls onto your stomach, and then pull back slowly, letting the heat and pressure ride down your body until it presses against your most intimate place like a tongue, and you start to pulse your hips beneath it. The water pressure is constant but as you move it breaks in different places, so that it never hits the same way twice, it finds new pathways down you, as insistent as a drum. You bite back a moan, and then think twice and let it go, listening to your pleasure echo in the tub's confines. You're tempted to reach your fingers down, to press them deep inside, but the water feels too good running on your clit – so instead you turn the faucet up, until the water's pounding you where fingers ought to be. You moan again, rocking your hips, looking at the angle of your legs inside the tub's stone and it's like you're one of the bathing statues down below, being fucked by an ancient and relentless deity, one that you know won't stop. The rest of the water sluices in the tub around you, grasping you like hot hands as you lift your hips up to meet the stream of water higher still, feeling it push into you and then roll up underneath your hood to tease at your clit – you take it for as long as you can stand, trembling on your toes as it roils down, pounding into your pussy, stroking along your folds, and sliding again and again over your clit like a lover's slick thumb.

The pleasure you were waiting for hits you like a wall. You cry out and your hips shake and your pussy clenches like it's trying to drink the water in.

You let out a long moan and fall back into the tub's basin, shuddering as the faucet keeps pouring out water over your suddenly ticklish thighs.

When you open your eyes again you see the ceiling over the tub, as white as that woman's porcelain skin.

Do you call for her? If so, go to page 13.

Or do you get dressed and go back outside? If so, turn to page 189.

She did say you could call her back at any time – you wish you knew her name.

You gather yourself and lean up in the tub. "Beautiful redheaded girl?" you say aloud, wondering if you can summon her like a genie.

Apparently you can, because a door you hadn't seen before at the back of the bathroom opens.

"Did you ring, Mistress?" she asks, peeking her head out with a grin.

You grin back, enjoying the tingle of possibility that you're beginning to feel. "I think I was wrong -- maybe I need help bathing after all."

Turn to page 14.

"Are you dirty?" she asks, not without innuendo, walking to the tub and leaning over to set the drain and faucet to allow two people. Her bathrobe falls open and you can see the curve of one small high breast, although the nipple is hidden.

"Sometimes," you say back, trying to play along. She smiles at this, and picks up another handful of the bath salts to sprinkle in the water beside you. Then she stands and unbelts her robe. She lets it fall to the ground at her ankles by the clothing you've already shed, and gestures you forward in the tub. You move to accommodate her, and she sinks in, sighing as the heat hits her just like you did prior. You can't see her behind you but you hear her pick something up and soon you feel a sponge wielded by expert hands against your back.

The sponge is real, one of those kinds only rich people can afford, and she scrubs at you, applying enough pressure to make your skin sing, lifting your hair out of the way to wash your neck. You feel her hands at your shoulders, your ribcage, your flank, and the top of your ass, small circles as she massages you clean. And when she is done with all of the skin she can reach she leans forward to whisper in your ear.

"Turn around."

You do so. It's a mark of how large this tub is that you can both comfortably face one another in it. Your legs are spread on either side of her and you would feel awkward if she weren't just as naked as you. She smiles and picks up your right hand and starts scrubbing at it, front and back. You can't help but notice that the water hits her at her nipple line and that her pubic hair is the same color as her hair only darker because it's wet.

She makes her way up one arm and then the other and then begins at your neck. You lift your chin up for her so that she can reach all of you and the circles slow down, becoming more precise as her hand washes down your chest. You're embarrassed at how quickly you start to breathe but you don't want to tell her to stop. The sponge scrapes gently at your breasts, leaving soft washes of red in its wake as she makes larger circles, cleaning more of your skin, careful not to touch your nipples which, oddly, makes them want to be touched more.

When she stops with a smile and then begins again at your feet, it's hard not to tell her to go back to where she was. You think you could order her to do so, and consider doing such, but as she washes and kneads her way up your calves, you discover you would rather find out what she has in mind.

She slows as she reaches your knees, washing one than the other, and then begins on your thighs, leading up in long strokes. Your lips part open, you think you know what is coming, but you both do and do not want to be sure. The not knowing is what makes it delicious you realize, as she rubs the rough sponge up your inner thigh. You lean back and she strokes up again, this time on the other, and there's no way not to gasp, hoping that she'll do more. Hearing this, she pauses and looks up at you. Her cheeks are as flushed as yours, and both of her nipples are hard and you realize that you're not the only one in this tub turned on.

"I have to clean all of you," she says in a breath.

"Yes, you do," you manage to say.

You're not entirely sure what to do, as you've never fucked a stranger in a strange tub before. But you know what feels good, and you lean forward. Her body slides up against yours, frictionless in the water, and you can feel her smooth skin pressed to yours in a thousand different places, as you kiss her on her full, soft, lips.

She kisses you back. Her lips are softer than a man's, more generous and sweet, and her tongue hesitates then kisses you ravenously. One of your hands holds you up, the other finds her neck, her breast, her skin. Her hand is at your ass, pulling you forward, your legs tangled together beneath the waterline. You set your knee down between her thighs and she gasps as she rubs her pussy on it.

She lets out a moan and rubs again, her pert breasts parting the waves. You lap at her nipples, drinking in as much water as air, and then they disappear, pulled down so she can grind herself harder into you. The water makes you float so that you have to fight to stay against her, and then her hand find the folds of your pussy and rubs against them, the slickness of your own body joining the slickness of the waves she makes, helping to anchor you down. You take the hand that isn't holding you up and plunge it down to meet her between her thighs, and touch her like she's touching you. She gasps and grinds again and you test pushing a finger inside of her. This makes her shudder – until she does the same to you, and then you're both caught on one another, twin mermaids being pulled out of the sea, rocking back and forth, pushing in, and then pulling out to rub against one another's clits. Her fingers pulse in time with the waves and you return the pleasure as you kiss her, her mouth, her neck, her breasts, and the pressure inside you mounts with each motion she makes, trapping you as you trap her, unable to think clearly anymore, skin against skin against skin against skin.

Her hand trembles inside of you, and you know from the expression on her face that she's almost there, that you've almost made her come in the palm of your own hand. You've kept your fingers deep inside of her but as she nears there's more space still and you push harder to find the depths of it, calling it out from her, watching her mouth part as her own hand rides deeper into you. You feel like you're drowning even though you're not. Looking down at her you see her lips parted with need, and her hips start to thrash at your hand, as her other hand pulls you close so that she can go deeper, pulsing frantically into you until you're both bucking, waves of water spilling out over the tub's edge until you both cry out half a second behind the other, not sure who came first, as waves of a different sort ripple through the water as your pleasure makes you thrash. Your moans and her moans fade and then there's only the sound of the water, slapping lightly against the tub's side, like an ass being slapped.

She smiles up at you, wide and earnest and it's impossible for you not to smile back. Then she stands before you in all of her naked glory, and steps out of the tub, grabbing a towel not for modesty's sake, but merely to dry off.

"See you soon, I hope," she says, and you feel she means it. You're unsure what to say back, but you rest your hands on the edge of the tub and watch her go. The only thing you're sure of now is that you want to know what the rest of the House has in store for you.

Do you go back out to the hallway? If so, turn to page 189.

Do you go to the back of the bathroom and listen at the door she disappeared behind? If so, flip to page 18.

*Y*ou stand and dry yourself off with one of the luxurious towels. Your clothing on the floor seems out of place against the rest of the bathroom so you pick a bathrobe up to put on. You cinch its silken tie around your waist and head to the back of the bathroom.

If you hadn't seen a woman walk though you wouldn't have known there was a door there, the seam is barely visible – the only thing that gives it away for sure is a tiny gold embossed escutcheon that you're sure will fit your silver key.

You hold your key up straight and press it in and turn and hear something deep inside the wall unlock. The marble spins like a mad scientist's bookcase in a movie, allowing you entry into a dark hall with a distant light. You take the key out and step in and the door slides shut behind you – and up ahead you hear two gasps.

Unable to find your way back now, you go towards the light at the end of the hall, where the gasping sounds are becoming low moans. Reaching the doorway, you feel safe again – inside the room everything's bathed in warm and welcoming light – including the two women making out on a massive white bed. White columns of fabric hanging from a vaulted ceiling hide the rest of the room's décor.

The redhead from before sees you first and startles, looking bashful. "I couldn't help myself, Mistress. I was still turned on."

The woman she was kissing has black features, dark hair, and full lips that she's using to smile indulgently at you. Underneath the sheets their legs are twined, and you don't see any hands.

Someone's hand slides under the sheets again at hip height and the redhead breathes roughly, still looking at you. "Mistress, is this where you want to be?"

Do you want to leave? If so, go to page 20.

Do you want to stay? If so, turn to page 23.

ou beat a hasty retreat back through the hallway to the bathroom where your clothes are still waiting. Pulling them on, you return out to the hall and find the butler waiting there.

"What's wrong?" he asks you, concerned.

"There were ladies," you say.

Both his eyebrows raise. "Aren't you…a woman?" he inquires, the soul of polite.

You make a face at him. "It's just that – I don't know what to do with them. I've never done anything like that before, not really."

He looks you dramatically up and down. "Mistress, if I may say so, you are possessed of your own operating manual. And I'm sure they'd be eager to help teach you, if you'd but ask."

You bite your lips, thinking.

"It is up to you though, as are all doors inside the House. You may choose another door entirely," he says, gesturing down the hall, "Or use tonight to stretch your imagination," he finishes, gesturing towards the white door behind him.

It might take you awhile to decide.

If you return to the purple door, turn to 193.

Or try the gray one? Try page 54.

If you'd like to go back into the white room with the women again, turn to page 21.

And walking down the hall you see a door you hadn't seen before – its color is eggshell blue, matching the sky of the nearest painting perfectly. If you want to listen at it, go to page 190.

ou realize you have nothing to be frightened of, really –
and the Butler's right. Tonight's your night to be brave
and bold.

You open up the white door and head into the bathroom, changing
back into your robe. Then you head to the back wall, use your key,
and walk back down the hidden hall.

"Mistress –" the redhead says, spotting you first. "We didn't mean
to –" she begins, and you wave your hand.

"Don't apologize," you say.

"I wasn't going to," the black woman says looking challengingly at
you, like you're something – someone – to be conquered, given half a
chance.

You sit down on the chair in front of their bed, like a queen taking
seat on her throne. "Please, continue."

The redhead casts another worried glance at you – but then whatever the black woman's doing beneath the sheets begins again, and she
now has her full attention.

You realize no mysteries will be solved this way, not when you
can't see anything. As the Mistress of the House, isn't it your right to
know what's going on? You walk to the bottom of the bed, their eyes
on you, their hips still rocking, and grab hold of the sheets that cover
them, and slowly pull them off.

It's like watching a distant portrait resolve itself, skin of dawn and
skin of dusk revealed, one pink set of nipples, the other cherry-wood
dark. Their breasts are rubbing against one another and their hands
are cupped into one another's crotch, thighs sliding on top of one
another as they do so.

Unaccustomed feelings stir inside you – jealousy, hunger, a deep-
ening ache.

The black woman does something more to make the redhead
moan. And then the redhead dives down to suck on the other
woman's breast and it's her turn to gasp out loud. You change seats to
be nearer, on the edge of the bed. You don't want to interrupt them
but you need to see what's going on. Your body needs to know.

The redhead kisses the black woman's breast while her hand is buried down where you can't see. But at the thought of having your own nipples sucked by her, or by the other woman – or maybe both at once -- urges light inside. You move even closer on the bed and your robe slides open over your thighs like an invitation to yourself.

Do you start touching yourself? If so, go to page 32.

If not, flip to page 182.

s you nod, the redhead's face flushes with relief. You're not sure what's in store here, but you definitely don't want to go. Her breath catches again, and you wonder what the darker haired woman is doing to her, hidden by the sheets.

"Please," the redhead says, and you're not sure who she's asking, you or the other woman. "Don't make her stop –" she says, breathing in with a hitch.

"Why would she make me stop when she can join?" The black woman looks back at you with hunger in her eyes.

Do you watch? If so, go to page 31.

Do you join? If so, turn to 24.

"*D*on't stop," you say, approaching the edge of the bed. The redhead moans again as the darker woman complies with your request. Watching them intertwined fills you with a longing to join them, but you don't know where to begin or how.

The black woman leans over and whispers something to the redhead, who blushes a little – hard, considering how flushed she already is. And then they both disengage, separating under the sheets from one another, and the black woman looks to you again.

"Come in," she says, tenting the sheet between them up, indicating that you should get inside. You mount the bed without thinking, and crawl in between them, tucking yourself in, facing the redhead, the Black woman behind you.

"We can take this off, right?" the redhead asks, and without waiting puts hands on your waist, undoing your robe's tie. You nod, and then the darker woman's at your back, pulling your robe down, silk sliding against silk, as your shoulders are exposed.

Hands start to brush you, and your own hands slide up. The redhead kisses you and your hand finds her waist, her back, her arm, her breasts. She gasps as your fingers stroke the supple weight of her, rolling a thumb over her nipple as her tongue touches yours. The darker woman's hands were on your waist but now they're curling up your ribs, coming for your breasts, as she licks up to the spot behind your ear, making you shudder. She purrs as she starts to massage at you, one breast in each hand. The redhead rocks forward to rub her breasts on yours, and you bend down to take her nipple into your mouth, feeling it harden instantly. She gasps and brings her hands up to your hair, scratching fingernails along your scalp.

The fabric of the sheets and the softness of so much skin makes sliding easy. You press down to catch the redhead's other breast in your mouth while massaging the first one, and feel her move one leg between your knees and you willingly spread your legs open. Hands and fingernails trail down your back along your spine as the black woman's breasts press up and then her hips move to grind against yours. You gasp, surprised at this more serious tone, and then you look up and twist backwards – and she bends forwards, matching your mouth with hers. You moan into her as she starts moving her hips against you, and as perfect as all of this is, you know what she wants – and you want it too. You move your own hips in time and find yourself grinding on the redhead's thigh. She purrs and reaches a hand down, lowering herself bodily, until her face is at the level of your breasts and she can easily slide her hand in where her leg used to be. You know what she's going to do and yet you gasp as she does it – her fingers find your clit and start to rub.

The darker woman bites your shoulder, and reaches through to grab your breasts again, as though she's both holding you still and presenting you to be touched. The redhead kisses your nipples and her fingertips work their way back to your labia, sliding across them with your own wetness, before pushing one into you, feeling your warmth, making you moan.

"But – I –" you feel helpless, like you're not doing enough for them, even though you are definitely enjoying what they're doing to you.

"Shh. You're the Mistress," the darker woman says, absolving you of guilt.

"You can always pay us back later," the redheaded woman says, looking up. Then she bites at your nipple playfully and moves her hand faster.

The black woman lets go of you with one arm and sinks it down. You think she's going to touch herself – but instead, she touches you. She traces it down your spine until she reaches your ass and grabs it roughly, almost growling in your ear. You lift your leg higher because that's what you think she wants and find it is – because her hand's now reaching at you from the back, middle and ring fingers diving inside your pussy, rubbing her thumb against your asshole.

You gasp and moan at so much new sensation, as the redhead presses another finger inside, and it's like they're both pulling you apart, setting formerly quiet nerves alight. The redhead's using two hands now, one in you, and one on your clit, and she's still sucking on one of your breasts, rolling your nipple against her tongue, and the black woman's licking and kissing on your back with an occasional unpredictable bite, and your hips start to wave, pinned by both of their desires for you to come between them, hard. You start to cry out as the tension builds, and the black woman bites you harder which turns you on more, and the redhead's fingers all speed up, and then the black woman slides her thumb inside your ass, and the sensations are all too much – your breath hitches, again and again and your hips thrust and their hands follow and your orgasm coils inside you like a spring until it explodes out of you with a shout.

You thrash between them, helplessly, crying out as you do so, listening to their moans of satisfaction at you coming on either side. You relax, feeling exhausted, even though you didn't put any effort in, and their hands come out.

"Was that good, Mistress?" the redhead asks.

"Do you need to ask?" you say, reaching a hand out to run through her hair.

She smiles mischievously at you.

"Now," the black woman says, propping herself up on an arm behind you. You look back, and her smile is positively wicked. "About paying us back….." She leans over the edge of the bed and pulls up two strap-ons from somewhere underneath it. "We have some ideas…."

Would you like to pay the black woman back first? If so, go to page 27.

Would you like to pay the redhead back first? If so, flip to page 29.

"Anything," you say.

"Anything?" the black woman challenges you.

A world of opportunities with her blossoms before you and you nod.

"I want to ride you," she says, handing the strap-on over. You haven't worn one before, but for her, and inside the House, you're willing to try. She helps you to put it on and soon there's a solid weight dangling between your legs, a purple silicone cock. It feels strange, but not bad, and when she pushes you down onto your back, you gladly roll.

She straddles your waist chastely, her long hair spilling down her chest, and you reach up to touch her breasts, her waist, her hips. From this angle she's even more beautiful than she was before – you had no idea that this was what it was like for men. Her torso is lean and her eyes are heavy and when she leans back you can cup her ass and it feels natural to bring your hips up into a line with hers. As she settles herself slowly onto the cock you have on, you have no idea why you've never done this before.

She moans as her pussy parts and takes you in, and you start to fuck her with slow even strokes. She smiles down, one hand on your chest one hand on her own, and you realize you could never get enough of this show, seeing her pinned above.

She reaches down and rubs at herself while you thrust up and down. You reach up and pinch a line on the insides of her thighs, hard enough to leave marks, and she gasps each time you do so. Her hand speeds up and so do you, trying to keep pace with her, watching her face as her jaw drops and she starts breathing hard, running your hands up her ribs to stroke her breasts and pull on her nipples.

She starts to lean forward, bouncing harder on you, and you take it and give it back to her, fucking her to the full extent the strap-on allows, pulling out and thrusting in in opposition to her so that you're going deep each time. Her hand moves faster and she starts to moan and curve forward – and you reach up to pull her down onto you, over you, stroking her from her back to her ass, bending your legs to fuck her madly, clutching her to your chest, her breasts rubbing against yours as you try to give her the orgasm she deserves. Her breath is hot in your ear and she starts to cry out and you redouble your efforts, slamming the cock into her, feeling her grind her hand between both of your clits, as she frantically tries to get herself off. You can feel her orgasm building inside of her, in the way she's holding on like you might buck her off, the growing tension of her ass and hips, the sweat sliding between both your chests -- you know she wants to come so badly – you slap her ass without thinking about it and she tenses over you, frozen in time except for her speeding hand, and then you slap her ass again, and it breaks the ice and she comes.

Her body shudders over you, the orgasm flowing through it like a tidal wave, from her hips to her shoulders, again and again. She cries out as it passes through her, her voice rising up and down like a buoy in a storm as you keep fucking her with your strap-on cock, until she collapses over you and gasps out a satisfied curse, and you begin to slow.

She lays there pressed against you and you bring your hands up her back, feeling the muscles there under her sweet soft skin, brushing away the sweaty skein of her hair. You lean down and kiss her forehead, and then after she lifts her head, her lips.

There's a polite throat clearing sound from the other half of the bed. She chuckles, and you look up to see the redhead giving you both a coquettish grin.

If you'd like to pay the redhead back, head to page 29.

If you notice a shadow inside a nearby column of fabric instead, try page 41.

ou turn towards the redhead. "What can I do?" you ask.

She moves towards you with the red strap-on that she holds. "This my favorite one."

You quickly put it on with her help and she smiles shyly, it's utterly charming.

"I just, sometimes," she says, laying down, "like an old-fashioned fuck."

It takes you a moment to catch her gist, to realize what she's offering you, then you nod. "Okay."

You lean over her, supporting yourself on your arms, and you kiss her first because that's what old-fashioned is about. You stare into her eyes and taste her strawberry lips as they part for your tongue, and you touch her breast and then work your hands down. Her legs part for you and you press fingers inside of her, feeling the wetness there, bringing them out to slide her juices along your thick silicone cock. She's ready, but are you?

"I've never – like this –" you say, because you haven't before.

"It's all right," she whispers, and reaches down to set your tip inside.

Your first thrust with the strap-on is slow and experimental, but she purrs as it goes in. You pull out, almost all the way, feeling the weight of the cock between your legs and the heaviness of her, before you slowly go back in again. You can feel the heat radiating from her as your own pussy nears, and she rises on her tip-toes to take more of you in.

After that it's easy to find a rhythm that pleases her – each thrust makes her sway in the bed and her eyes close as she moans. You lean over to kiss her breasts, supporting your weight off of her with your hands, and then her hands are at your back, clawing her fingernails down. You gasp at this, surprised, shocked, and even more turned on.

"I want you to come," you say before you can think saying such things through. Her eyes open, focusing on you, and she nods.

"I want that too –" she says, as you lower yourself over her, so that your hips can do closer, faster work. Her hand slips between you both and you can feel her start to rub.

It's not just about you here anymore, it's about you and her, and you want to make her come so hard, hear her shout in your ear, and know that you're the one that made it happen. The cock between your legs slides solidly into her, again and again, and you move faster as her hand speeds up, as her breathing begins to turn into one long moan.

"Just like that –" she gasps, and you can feel her start to tense. You arc your hips up at the end of the next thrust, and she groans again – "Oh -- just like that – like that – " she gasps and you know she's almost come undone. You growl in concentration and in hunger for her body to be satisfied – her free hand reaches up to clutch into your hair and wind and your hips are smashing her hand in over her clit as you ride her hard.

"Please," she gasps out, and so you don't stop, you can't. She cries out, a small sharp sound, followed by a low moan, as she moves beneath you like a wave. Her breasts bob up as another pulse arcs through her, and then a third, until she cries out again, and falls back to the bed, spent. You thrust one last time, marveling at the strange connection between you and her, and then pull slowly out.

If you'd like to pay the black woman back, go to page 27.

If you notice a shadow inside a nearby column of fabric instead, flip to page 41.

"*D*on't stop," you say. You're not sure about joining in yet though, not until you're sure what you're getting in to. You walk to the bottom of the bed, their eyes on you, their hips still rocking, and grab hold of the sheets that cover them, and slowly pull them off.

It's like watching a distant portrait resolve itself, skin of dawn and skin of dusk revealed, one pink set of nipples, the other cherry-wood dark. Their breasts are rubbing against one another and their hands are cupped into one another's crotch, thighs sliding on top of one another as they do so.

Now that everything is visible, it's starting to make you ache.

"Definitely don't stop," you say.

The black woman chuckles and does something more to make the redhead moan. And then she dives down to suck on the black woman's breast and it's her turn to gasp out loud. You take a seat on the edge of the bed, not wanting to interrupt, but to see close up just what's going on.

The redhead kisses the black woman's breast again while her hand is buried down where you can't see. But at the thought of having your own nipples sucked by her, or by the other woman – or maybe both at once -- urges light inside. You move closer on the bed and your robe slides open over your thighs like an invitation to yourself.

Do you start touching yourself? If so, go to page 32.

If not, turn to page 182.

ou slide your hand up your own thigh, pulling the robe back up. You don't want them to see you yet, which might be unfair considering that they're both so exposed – but you're the one with the key, aren't you?

The black woman moves to be the one on top, while the redhead casts a glance back at you – until the black woman kisses her collarbone and her eyes close in cat-like bliss. She arches her ribs up, presenting her chest to be kissed, and black hair spills over porcelain white skin as the black woman obliges. Her mouth detours towards one breast, nuzzling and kissing it, while her hand massages the other, rolling erect nipples between thumb and forefinger, pinching hard enough to make the redhead gasp. Her mouth suckles, pulling the redhead's nipples taut inside, and she lifts her lips enough so that you can see her using her teeth for sharper kisses at the end. Her eyes lift and meet yours knowingly and you can only think one thing – that she's showing you how she wants to be fucked.

Hands still on the redhead's breasts, the black woman bends down as if in prayer, drawing a line on the other woman's stomach, kiss after kiss. The redhead goes still, her breathing transformed into panting, tensed in anticipation – and you find your breath matching hers. Your hand sinks between your own legs, stroking the robe up your thigh to bunch against your pussy, and you wait just like she waits for what you know has to come –

The black woman's tongue finds the redhead's pussy and she lets out a whine just as you start stroking yourself through the fabric of the robe. Her hands are still on the redhead's breasts, rubbing them with broad strokes, just as broad as you imagine her tongue is on the redhead's clit. The redhead's back is arched and her head is thrown back, eyes still closed. She can't see you touching yourself, but the black woman can. You rock back to show more of yourself to her, as if offering her another dish – you know you said you didn't want to join earlier, but that was before seeing this.

The redhead's hips start to pulse and the black woman moves a hand in and you know fingers are disappearing into the redhead's wet folds. You start stroking yourself faster in response, imagining her hand inside you instead, and as the redhead starts crying out, not in orgasm but close, unable to help herself, you feel your own pussy start to clench.

You pull the fabric of your robe aside so that you can feel flesh on flesh. The redhead's voice is louder now, you can tell the other woman's hand and mouth are bringing her to the brink, and you're determined to go with her, you need this as badly as she does. The darker woman's eyes are hot on you – you started off wanting to watch her, and now you want to make her watch you. You're rubbing yourself so hard, hips quaking, toes on pointe, moments away, as she orchestrates the redhead's inevitable demise, the sound of hands sliding wetly and mouths sucking and the redhead's whines as she desperately tries to come and not come, holding onto the moment longer, sharp, hot, sweet –

The redhead can't take it any longer and screams out. Her whole body shakes as the orgasm runs through her like she's been struck by lightning. The black woman follows the redhead's hips through with her mouth, and it's thinking of that that makes you come, the thought of her mouth clasped against your pussy, her tongue probing, her fingers pushed inside – seeing it and dreaming it and knowing you can make it happen soon -- the last of the redhead's moans call your orgasm from you, from your hips up through your mouth, making you roil on the bed with a hissing gasp. When you still, the redhead reaches out and companionably takes hold of your ankle, smiling up – and the black woman rocks back onto her knees looking smug, as though she's conquered both of you, because maybe she has.

She crawls across the bed towards you, hair draped down in a black sheet, and you know you have only seconds to decide what you want next.

If you want to eat her out try page 35.

If you want her to eat you, turn to page 39.

$\mathcal{S}$he looks like a cat as she pads closer, like she's made one kill and is hungry for a second, the other woman's scent hot on her breath.

But that's not what you want from her right now. You rise up and look at her.

"Lay down," you say.

She looks confused for a moment, and disheartened, but she does as you command.

You move to kneel beside her, resting a fluttering hand on her knee, and wonder if she can feel how fast your heart is beating through it. You haven't done this much before, there was that one time in college, but that hardly counts – you lean over her and kiss her, just like she kissed the redhead earlier.

Her lips are softer than any man's as they part, fuller, sweeter – but the hands that sweep up to play in your hair and tilt your face, pulling you close, hold just as much need as a man's -- just as much need as you do. It occurs to you though that need is universal, and you know what you're going to do.

You do what you saw her do with the redhead, mimicking her kiss by kiss. The angle of her chin where it meets her throat, down her exquisite collarbone, onto the flat bone between her breasts, and then out to them, massaging and rubbing one while flicking your tongue over the other. Her nipples are tender in your mouth, and you suck at them, feeling her body start to come alive beneath you, hips starting to push up, chest heaving higher, trying to give you more of her flesh. Inside your mouth her nipples become tight like little erasers, and you play your tongue back and forth on one while rubbing the other, and then nip lightly, ever so lightly, with your teeth, just like you saw she'd done. She whines at this, her breathe catching in her throat – and then you start kissing down.

You kiss down to the flat pit of her stomach and continue on, feeling her knees part beneath you as she spreads herself wide. You move to kneel in front of her and can see the folds of her labia like unfurled flower petals, and the soft flesh of her hood hiding her clit, and before you can pause and get scared about what you're going to do next, you lean down and kiss her there.

It's a soft kiss, unsure, but you know where you like to be licked and touched – and she gasps as you go in again. You realize she's been holding her breath, afraid that you might change your mind – and so you kiss her again, this time more wetly.

Two more kisses, and the kisses become licks, as you drag your tongue up her, moving her hood to expose the clit underneath. She shivers and moans, and the redhead, watching both of you, moves in to kiss her throat, putting hands on both her breasts, leaving you to navigate the known yet unknown space between her thighs.

You lick her softly, slowly working your way down her pussy until your tongue presses her labia open, exposing the her slickness inside. She's wet, turned on by you and from her turn eating out the redhead, and she tastes hot, salty, sweet. You dab your tongue at her afraid of doing the wrong thing, until you realize there's no way to do anything wrong – so you lick her harder, pressing your tongue in, feeling the softness of her give way. She moans again, and it makes you bold -- you reach up with a hand and pull the skin over her pubic bone higher, so that the hood over her clit's pulled back, and concentrate there, kissing, licking, sucking, listening to the way she breathes, the moans she makes, the way her hips start to involuntarily quiver. When you kiss her *there* her breath hitches, and when you suck her just *so* she gasps – and when you press your tongue into her pussy as far as it can go she makes a sound like half a scream. You scoot higher so you can concentrate on her clit while bringing your free hand up between her legs.

You slide a finger inside of her and she feels like you do the times you've felt yourself, wet and warm and perfect. You circle it around and feel her move as you do so, wet flesh sliding over flesh, and you keep your head bowed, tongue lapping at her as you slide another finger in, so that your middle and ring fingers are knuckle deep, and then you crook your fingers inside and rub the spot you find there as her pussy starts to tense against you.

She shudders and you moan just as she does, turned on by the thought of bringing her off. Her hips throb in time with the motion of your hand and you keep your mouth on her, as if you're trying to suck the juice out of a peach – when the redhead moves.

The redhead slides a hand down your back so that you know she's there, you can feel it stroke down your spine and then near the cleft of your ass, holding onto one cheek, before resting on the back of one of your thighs, and you know what she is asking of you. You spread your legs without thinking, and she chuckles, settling her hand in. She pushes her thumb into your pussy, finding you eager and wet, and then starts stroking on your clit with the first two fingers of her same hand.

You gasp, and the black woman looks down, sees what the redhead is doing, and then smiles wickedly, before throwing her head back again. You lick faster, using the tip of your tongue against her clit, as the redhead presses her thumb against the entrance of your pussy, making it stretch in the most delightful way. You groan, and the redhead purrs, and the darker woman's pussy starts to warm and tighten, pressing harder against your pulling fingers. You slide a third finger into her and she shudders bodily. You want her to come – you want her to come more than you do yourself, although you're sensitive because you're already so turned on and the redhead's fingers won't stop – you move your fingers faster, trying to coax her before you lose control –

She reaches down and winds her hands in your hair pulling your face into her, holding you just where she needs you to be as she starts to cry out. You lick and suck and roll and rub, pulsing your fingers inside of her pussy. Her voices rises as the orgasm you're giving her begins, and you feel it as she clenches around your fingers, hot waves matching the quaver in her voice. She curls forward, panting, and you ride her through, desperate to pull even the end of her orgasm out of her, unwilling to leave any part of her behind. She lets go of your hair, then collapses back against the bed with a gasp.

It's safe then for you to concentrate on the redhead's ministrations. Her thumb winds in you and her fingers slide over your clit, and watching the black woman come because of you was maybe the hottest thing you've ever seen – it made you want to come with her, and so you raise your hips and moan as the redhead's hand speeds up – you're close now, your body tensing, breasts pressed against the sheet, feeling tight and yet so very open – your hips bob and your pussy clenches tight around her rubbing hand and she purrs knowing what's about to come next -- you shout out as you start coming, hard. Her hand follows you, rubbing you as you pulse against her, drawing the last of your orgasm out longer than it has any right to be, until you collapse on the bed in between the darker woman's perfect legs.

She leans up and over and down to kiss you, the taste of her own juices still on your lips, and then she kisses the redhead, and all three of you are in a tangle of limbs and possibility.

"Ready for more?" she asks you, when you can breathe again.

The only answer you can give is, "Yes."

Turn to page 41.

ou know what you want – there's no way you couldn't want it, not after seeing the redhead writhe.

"Please," you breathe out, showing yourself to her.

She gets a wicked smile – and then lowers her head. Not onto your pussy, like you were praying for, but on the inside of your knee. Her hair falls over your leg like the brush of a cat's tail and she starts very deliberately kissing up the inside of your thigh. You make a noise as she starts to torture you slowly, a sound of hunger and fear, the pain of waiting, the agony of suspense. Her perfect mouth raises up and then down again, a fraction of an inch at a time, leaving a wet trail on you behind her lips, one that cools as she moves up, slower, and slower, and slower, until you're aching so badly you can hardly stand it. You move a hand to touch yourself without thinking, but then the redhead's there, shaking her head and catching your wrists to keep you still. You look up into her clear blue eyes, wishing you could kiss her lips, as the black woman's lips near your folds and you can feel her breath and wait-wait-wait until her kiss is on your clit, and you gasp out a sigh. She makes an appreciative noise as she starts to lick at you, and you shudder.

You've never – it's never been quite like this before – you watch her working on you and it's almost as hot as feeling her lip's touch, and then you look up and see the redhead, chest heaving. The darker woman's tongue presses inside of you and you moan, then she goes back to stroking your clit with her tongue's tip, finding the place that you know will drive you wild.

The redhead's hand on you relents, distracted as she's turned on. She takes her hand off of yours and moves it down to touch herself instead, rubbing her own clit as the black woman's tongue rubs yours.

With your newly freed hands, you reach down your own body, stroking your own skin along the way, until you can run your fingers into the darker woman's hair. She purrs as you do so, and you wind your fingers, until you're pulling on her long black hair like reins, as your hips arch up. Her tongue doesn't stop, it won't stop, not until she's made you come – the redhead whines and you look over at her, even though she just came, she wants to come again, with you. The bed is rocking with need, and you know you're so close, there's no way you could be closer – then the black woman stops, leaving you hanging on the edge.

You pant, looking down as she looks up at you.

You could order her to start up again – but being helpless is its own special kind of turn on.

"Please," you whisper again, breathlessly. She smiles indulgently up at you, and then her cat-eyes sink as her head bobs back down.

You let go of her hair then and move to hold onto the sheets on either side of you – you know by asking for it that one last time that there's no way you're not going to come, she's going to take you to the edge and push you off of it.

Her tongue starts speeding up, rubbing against your clit, stroking all of it, around and across and up and down. You can't tell where one sensation ends and the next one begins, all of you is so turned on and everything she does feels so fucking good. Your heels rise up, your calves tense, your stomach goes stiff and she won't relent, she won't stop pushing you, pressing you, licking you, owning you – you cry out, hips thrashing as you fuck her mouth. Your orgasm wrenches through you, feeling like it might pull you apart – and beside you the redhead starts to whine, her voice rising as she nears a cliff of her own. Just as you sag back down she comes, the sound of her orgasm beginning where yours leaves off.

You lay sprawled in bed, completely wrung out.

"What now?" you ask, unwilling for things to be over, but otherwise unable to form a complete thought.

The darker woman smiles at you. "Now, for round two," she says.

Turn to page 41.

he darker woman rises and gets up off the bed. You look to see where she's going – and you're almost sure you saw a hint of a shadow inside one of the opaque white columns nearby.

"What is that?" you ask, convinced you're seeing things.

The darker woman grins, takes the fabric in one of her hands, and tugs. The column flutters down from the ceiling – to drape itself over a tan blindfolded man, kneeling inside.

You and the redhead gasp – you were being spied on this whole time! But – he has a blindfold on, and was inside fabric besides, you know he couldn't really see you. He definitely heard everything though – you know, because he's completely naked, which makes it easy to see his erection.

"He's here for us to use how we see fit, Mistress. If you choose to use him, that is," she says, smiling at you. "We were doing fine on our own, after all."

You bite your lower lip in thought. There'd be so much you could do with an extra mouth and pair of hands, not to mention his cock. Several different options play out inside your mind, and you lean back on the bed with the redhead to consider them.

IF YOU WANT to pull him up onto the bed with you, try page 45.

If you want to make him listen to you all again, turn to page 42.

*Y*ou get a torturous idea. For him at least – not the three of you.

You look to the other two women and grin, then put a finger to your lips, before getting on all fours and making an orgasmic groan.

The redhead's face lights up, catching onto your game, and she gasps seductively. The darker woman chuckles low and then sighs as though someone has just stroked up her thigh.

You groan again, and the redhead cups a hand to her mouth to stop her from laughing. You almost laugh yourself – until the black woman smacks your ass, sending a genuine crack through the room.

You turn back to look at her and she raises both hands. The sound was real, wasn't it? And it's not like the man listening in knows any better. You waggle your hips, inviting her to smack it you again, and she does, harder this time, rocking you forward – and making you gasp.

The redhead bounces up to all fours to present her own bottom – and you take the opportunity to hit it, open palmed, leaving a rising red handprint against her porcelain skin. She groans for real this time, and you're getting turned on again. You stroke your hand over her ass, feeling her flinch and then lean in. You raise your hand again and then lower it, until she looks back at you, eyes asking you to spank her – so you do, and she hisses through gritted teeth – and arches back at you for more like a cat.

You spank her again and again, man forgotten, listening to her pant and whine. Red handprints are defined and then combine into indescribable patterns, until her entire ass is red and she's breathing hot.

She collapses on the bed in front of you, and you think you've maybe pushed her too far, but then you see her hips roll forward and her hand sink down between her legs – and you know what you want next.

You sink down on the bed, face up, and reach for her hips. She turns, unsure until she sees the look on your face and the way you lick your own lips and moves to straddle you in an instant, knees wide on either side of your head, sinking her pussy down onto your willing mouth. You press your tongue up into her folds and taste her, salty and sweet, and reach up with both hands to grab hold of her sore ass, radiating off freshly-spanked heat.

Is the man's heart racing? Does his cock hunger? You no longer care. The world narrows down to the magnificent creature above you, how she tastes, how she smells, how you can bring her off. You lick at her hard and fast as her hips begin to pulse and legs spread even wider, eager to give herself to you.

And then you feel a hand on the inside of your thigh. The black woman's there, kissing the redhead as she rides your face, and her hand is stroking up to where you know you're already wet. You moan into the redhead's pussy as her fingers slide into you and you feel her start to fuck you with her hand.

Eating the redhead out has made you too turned on for your own good – it's hard to concentrate on her anymore when the darker woman's thumb starts to rub against your clit, and over you both of them are kissing, groaning, pawing at each other's breasts where you can see. The redhead's ass starts to clench beneath your hands, her hips shaking with the need to come your tongue has lit inside her, and you know just what to do –

You spank her. Your hand slaps her ass, over the other handprints left there earlier, and you know it burns. It drives her pussy harder into your waiting tongue, shoving her clit against it. She cries out, so close to coming, and you spank the other cheek and it pushes her over the edge. Her hips roil against you, grinding down, taking what she needs from your mouth.

Seeing her come, feeling her come, her juices dripping down, makes your own pussy clench around the darker woman's hand. She fingerfucks you hard in response, her thumb rubbing against your clit each time and within seconds you're screaming helplessly into the redhead's pussy.

The redhead carefully moves off of you and then collapses, and you lay there prone and panting, covered in another woman's scent.

The black woman kneeling nearby looks over at you, as if to make sure you didn't fuck yourself to death.

"You're right, we didn't need him," you tell her.

She laughs and grins. "True. But he still might be fun."

Turn to page 45.

ou spend a full minute contemplating different ideas and gathering yourself. And then you grin wickedly at the black woman. "Bring him here."

She takes his shoulder gently, guiding him up to stand. He walks to the bed unable to see, but willing – his eager cock is clearly ready. His legs hit the bed's edge and you take his hand to pull him onto it. He goes to all fours and crawls to where you pull him, moving him to the center of the bed where you push him down, rolling him onto his back so he's prone.

The key to the House dangles on your wrist, forgotten in earlier revelry. He can't see -- how would he know who you are and what you mean to this place without it? You press it down into his nearest palm.

"Do you know who I am?" you whisper. His fingers grab the key then release it and he nods. "Good. Do what we want, and I promise you will be rewarded."

He licks his lips and nods again. You stroke his chin and you know he has just enough stubble to pleasantly chafe, and consider it. Then again there's his hard cock, still straining and hopeful.

Would you like to sit on his face? If so, turn to page 49.

Would you rather sit on his cock? If so, go to page 46.

ou reach a hand out to stroke his cock once and watch him shudder. He's so helpless – and so hungry. You give a meaningful glance to the redheaded woman and then to his face and that wonderfully stubbled chin.

"Gladly," she says and moves to mount him. He can feel the bed change around him as she does so, so he has to know what's going on – you watch his jaw drop as her pussy nears and in your hand you feel his hard-on twitch.

She moans as his lips touch her and you can see his chin move as he kisses her clit and hear the soft sucking sound as he plays with her labia before he starts to use his tongue. She leans forward, arching her back in pleasure.

His cock is hot under your hand – probably just as hot as his tongue is. Without thinking you swing your hips over his and rub your wet pussy along his shaft. His hands reach for your thighs and grab them, begging you, as his mouth works harder at the other woman's clit.

You lean forward, reach down, and set his tip in, and feel him try to thrust.

"Behave," you chide him. Then you remember everything he's been through, trapped listening to the three of you, and decide to take pity on his poor hungry cock.

You slide down him at once, taking all of him in. He almost shouts, muffled by her pussy, as you start to fuck.

Even though he can't see you his body knows what to do – as does yours. You reach out for the redhead and she twists back to kiss you. The other woman leans near you both and starts kissing lips, stroking your backs, and pinching at your nipples.

You lean forward, sliding his cock in and out, enjoying the feel of it and realize how nice it is in this moment to be divorced from kindness, to just get to take what you want.

The darker woman kisses the redhead and you see her dart her hand down to play with herself while watching the three of you. You take the man's cock deep and grind yourself onto him, hearing him groan, feeling him tense, watching the redhead's back arch as he translates that satisfaction into licking her – and then you start riding him low, rubbing your clit against the smooth skin above his cock.

His cock stiffens inside of you, sensing your change – it's not about teasing anymore, it's about getting off. Your hips make the bed sway and you watch his fingers curl against the redhead's thighs, holding her tighter onto him so that he can lick out every last drop inside her. She crouches forward, hands winding in the sheets, her voice a rising moan. Then inside of you his cock finds that one hard-soft spot that feels the best and you drop lower and grind harder and ride him into the bed like you are using him up –

The redhead comes first but only barely, her moan turning into a shout, thrusting her hips down to rub more of his tongue and he thrusts at this, unable to help himself – and it sends you reeling. You give a guttural scream as your own hips madly thrash, your pussy clenched around his cock like a hand.

The redhead sags forward and rolls to one side, off of him.

"Mistress," the man says with a gasp, licking his lips clean of her wetness, his cock still rock hard inside of you.

"Go," you say, letting go of his hands, changing to hold onto the bed instead for the ride you know is about to come.

His hands reach for your hips blindly, and your pussy's still sealed around his cock. Now that he can move he takes you fiercely, hard, pulling his legs under him so that he can thrust up into all of you – his hands move up your body to pull you down and cradle you against his chest, fucking you desperate and fast, like he's afraid you'll change your mind. His cock slams into you and his breath is ragged and you feel him tense and he shouts as his load leaves him, shooting deep inside of you.

You stay against his chest for a moment, breathing hard, and then rise up slowly with the feeling that tomorrow – whenever that manages to be -- you will be deeply and pleasurably sore. And then you collapse onto the bed by the redheaded woman's side.

There's so many other things in this room that all of you could do – but the House is large, and there could be so many other interesting doors….

Turn to page 52.

he possibilities of a blindfolded man with an erection are almost endless. It's hard to decide – but decide you do. You reach out and run your fingers through his short sandy-brown hair and lower your mouth to his ear.

"Are you good with your tongue?" you ask him, breathing warmly on his neck.

"Very," he promises.

You move yourself to straddle his face, and slowly bob yourself down. It's awkward feeling to do this without seeing his eyes, but as your pussy nears and his lips open to take you in, the stubble of his cheeks barely scratching your thighs, you begin to feel you've made the right choice. And with the first exploratory lick of his tongue on your clit his fate is sealed.

You sigh and set yourself further down, giving him space to move his jaw and chin as he starts kissing you, his tongue stroking up between your folds and underneath your hood to find your clit. Your breath catches and you lower yourself a little more – and he starts to press inside your pussy with his tongue, working against the tight muscles he finds there.

A hand reaches up to grab hold of your thigh – and another one reaches behind you so that he can touch himself.

"Not so fast," the darker woman chides.

"Not unless the Mistress says you can," the redhead teases.

His breath is hot against your thighs as he eats you – but looking over your shoulder, it does seem like a shame to let his hard-on go to waste.

"You should – if you want to --" you suggest, to both of them. They look from one another, and the redheaded woman bites her lip.

"If I have too," she says, her protest obviously fake, as she tosses a lean leg over him.

You know she's taken his cock inside herself when he stops licking you to shudder. You chuckle and look down at him with a tsk. "What's been given can be taken away again."

He moans – and his tongue starts working at you with a vengeance.

The redhead takes hold of your hips like an anchor and makes the entire bed rock with the force of her thrusts on his cock. The darker woman's beside you both, reaching in to kiss your shoulders, pinch your nipples, touching herself too. His lips tug at your labia and his tongue strokes your clit before pressing in – you spread your legs wider, sinking even further down, taking him inside. His chin rubs against your inner thighs his beard deliciously scraping against you with every movement that he makes – and then he starts nibbling at your clit again, sucking at it like it's an offered grape, taking all of your clit and hood into his mouth alone, his chin pressing up into your pussy hard. Your voice becomes otherworldly as the weight in your hips builds to a fevered point, ready to shout as he takes one last long suck -- you scream out roughly, just one long raw sound.

Then the redhead's fingers claw down your back as she comes, and the sudden pain squeezes your orgasm out longer than it has any right to be. You fall onto your arms and dismount his face like he's a horse, before laying back down on the bed. The redheaded woman does the same thing, only on the other side. The darker woman's at the head of the bed out of the way now -- and up between all of you is still his hard cock.

You make a gesture and offer him to the darker woman, but she shakes her head.

"Not my style," she says. Then you look back to the redhead, hands up in a question.

She makes a show of pondering things, and then grins. "Sure. Why not?"

She turns to crawl over him, down his body, so that her knees are on either side of his head and her mouth is right above his cock.

The redhead settles herself onto him at both spots simultaneously, so that just as her pussy lights down over his mouth, her mouth takes his cock in. He groans into her and raises his hands up to run along her side. The redhead gives you a knowing look as she sucks and you already know what he can do with his tongue. His hips are begging to thrust into her mouth as she arches and you decide to release him.

Moving to the head of the bed you reach between her legs to his face and you tug the blindfold down. Surprised blue eyes look up, and you mouth one unmistakable word.

"Come."

He groans into her pussy and starts writhing beneath her, desperate to feel her orgasm wash over him so that he can give her his in return. He curls up, licking at her hard, reaching a hand up to press a thumb into her darkest spot and she gasps and whines while still gagging on him. They writhe together, each hungrily taking what they can, an endless machine of mated desire -- she lifts up off of him for one arching second, ass up like a cat, mouth wide, about to shout – and her orgasm flips inside her like a switch and she bows down again, screams muffled by the cock she's letting him thrust inside.

He holds onto her until she's done, but then presses his feet down so that he can rise up and take more of her mouth. You see his balls tighten and hear him groan, until he thrashes beneath her, again and again, him bucking and her taking it, until he collapses beneath her, completely spent.

She rises up, shaky after her own orgasm, and looks back at you, a thin line of silvery cum leaking from one corner of her lips, like a cat caught drinking milk.

You look down at the man. "Feeling rewarded?" you ask him, one eyebrow arched.

"Very," he gasps out, reaching up to pull his blindfold back down.

The night still feels young. It's tempting to stay here, but you know there are more doors waiting to be opened outside. You kiss both women and then stand, naked now except for your dangling key, and walk back to the bathroom at the end of the hall.

Turn to page 52.

You head back to the bathroom and wash yourself up. With great reluctance you put your clothing back on.

Luckily you have a feeling it won't be staying on for long.

Turn to page 53.

When you emerge into the hallway, it feels full of opportunity.

The same doors are there as before, as is the butler, waiting politely.

Would you like to open the purple door with men's voices behind it? If so, turn to page 193.

There's still a bath being drawn behind the white door. If you'd like to visit it, go to page 9.

The gray door still has the sound of rope rubbing over other rope, turn to page 54.

And walking down the hall you see a door you hadn't seen before – its color is eggshell blue, matching the sky of the nearest painting perfectly. If you want to listen at it, flip to page 190.

ou stand outside the gray door, tempted but shy. The butler comes near looking concerned.

"Mistress?" he prompts you, his voice low.

"You promise everything will be fine?" you ask this man who you've never met before tonight.

He brings a formal hand to his chest. "More than that. I give you my word." There's something in the tone of voice he uses. You feel, deep down inside, that he means what he promises.

You listen again. It's definitely rope sliding over rope in there. The thought of being tied up – or tying someone else up – excites you, but you're afraid. Who in their right mind wouldn't be?

You look over at the butler. "Will you come with me?"

His eyebrows rise, surprised by your request, but then he nods before bowing again. "If it is what my Mistress wishes, then I must."

Somehow feeling safer with him on your side, even if you know that sounds insane, you put your key inside the gray door's lock.

Turn to page 55.

he room behind the gray door is large, and covered in luxurious furnishings, but the lighting is dim – mostly candlelight, you realize, seeing flickers of flames at the outskirts.

"Subs are always blindfolded. Say 'red' if you want anything to stop," the butler tells you, and you nod.

There's a wide open space in the center of the room and a wooden construction over it, like a four poster bed with extra cross beams. A naked and blindfolded woman's been ornately hung from this. You gasp at seeing her and walk near. Rope ties her at regular intervals, braided across both of her legs, wrapping up her torso in an intricate series of netted knots, windowing both of her breasts, and then flowing out again over her arms, suspending her at at least ten different points back up to the beams. The ropes follow the curves of her body, portioning her out for display, her legs spread wide, showing her off like she's been trussed up by a spider with an appreciation for female anatomy.

There's a man there too, wearing jeans, no shirt, with well-muscled arms. His face is intent with concentration, tying the final knot. When he's done he slaps her ass, and her body sways, ropes creaking against wood and flesh, and she groans around the gag in her mouth – more rope. You almost say something, afraid for her safety – then you notice the drying spots on the ground beneath her pussy, where the wetness of her excitement has rained down.

You glance over at the butler who's standing in the shadows, and the man tying knots finally notices you.

"Mistress," he says, and gives you a curt nod. You may be in charge of the House, but you're not completely the boss of him.

"What's going on here?" you ask. The woman's blonde hair sheets down from above as she follows your voice.

"Touch her and see," he says with pride.

You reach up and feel her breast. It's hot, and there's a line of red where the rope's triangled around it, gravity making her nipple point down. You run your thumb over its point, swollen and pink, and her breath catches. Was that a good thing? Maybe, but -- you reach out for her blindfold. Pushing it up, she blinks at you with blue eyes, expression blissed out as though she's taken a drug, but she's smiling, lips curving up on either side of the gag.

The man smacks her ass again, making her sway, and she moans.

"What is it like?" you ask him, since she can't answer.

He surveys his handiwork, eyes gauging the hanging woman's reaction. "Rope pulls everything tight, makes blood rush out, lights up each nerve." He reaches up into the woman's hair, stroking it out of her face again, and she looks adoringly down at him. He's in charge of her fate right now, you realize, and she likes it. "Rope teaches you what it is to control and be controlled," he goes on.

"I want that," you say before you can think twice.

Tearing his eyes off of her for you, the corner of his lips lifts up in a smirk. "Which part?"

Do you want to control? Turn to page 57.

Do you want to be controlled? Try page 67.

"*T*each me."

The man grins at this. "Done."

He holds up a hand and snaps his fingers twice, and out of the dimness across the room, a new man appears, also in jeans and a blindfold. He walks over to you both, apparently by echolocation, and kneels. Chin-length hair covers half of his blindfold. He has broad shoulders and a swimmer's back, and you realize if you're supposed to hoist him up --

"Am I – no way –" you say, looking from the new man to the woman overhead.

The dom laughs, shaking his head. "Hanging her took hours -- I'm sure you want to visit other doors. But this will be fast, and he's ready."

"Is he?"

"Ask him yourself."

You kneel and raise his blindfold. His eyes are a dark liquid brown and his lips part as he sees you. "Mistress," he whispers.

"Why are you here?" you ask him.

"So that you can do whatever you want with me."

You lick your lips. He's beautiful. You could think of a lot of things to want with him. The dom looks down at you like he knows what you're thinking – and the allure of doing what he does comes into sharp focus.

"Show me," you say, as he hands you a length of rope.

"Hold your hands behind your back," he orders, and the sub does.

The dom's hands are over yours, his body rubbing up against you as he shows you what to do, and where to knot. He smells like sweat, and the sub smells like soap, and with both of them this near it's easy to forget the woman overhead and the butler standing in the background watching in.

Together with the dom you pull ropes tight against the man's arms, starting at the shoulder and working your way down to his wrists. The dom shows you how not to rope burn the man, and stops you from pulling tight enough to cut off circulation, how to find the sweet spot between pain and control and not veer into harm. When the framework is done, you thread rope through it like a corset, and cinch his arms behind him, tying the ends of the rope into a knotted bow. The dom shows you which one to pull to free him quickly, just in case.

The sub is still kneeling, but he's trussed now, helpless before you. There was no way a woman your size could control a man as strong as him just seconds ago, but now he's utterly reliant on you. You realize whatever you wish, he would have to obey. It's intoxicating – and not just for you. The jeans the sub is wearing clearly show the outline of his hard cock.

"And now you see, Mistress," the dom says, with another bow. "If you'll forgive me, I have to take her down."

You nod quickly and he undoes a key series of knots overhead. Ropes fall from the woman and he catches her, sliding her down his body to the ground. She's shaky as a newborn fawn, pressed up against his side, and he picks her up easily. Putting her over his shoulder, he walks out a hidden back door, leaving you, your sub, and the butler alone.

"What now?" you ask the man you've bound.

"Now is up to you," he says, his voice low.

You want to use the sub, and he wants to be used – it seems fair enough. And there's a weight building inside of you that needs to be relieved.

You glance up at the butler. "Don't look," you say, and you see his eyes close.

You stroke a hesitant hand through the sub's hair, and put another one on his chest. He can't return your affections with his arms tied behind him, which is freeing – all of the touches this encounter will be yours. You take his blindfold fully off though, you want to see his face and eyes, especially as you reach down to put your hand there, right over his straining cock.

This is your chance to take what you want from him, no questions asked.

You lean in over him. "Say red if you want anything to stop," you whisper, just as you were told, and then you press him down and onto his back.

You don't even take his jeans all the way off – just down to his knees, far enough so that he can move his thighs. Since his hands are trapped beneath him, everything is up to you.

You lean over, mouth open, and he gasps in hope, but instead of taking him into your mouth, you breathe on him instead. He makes a disappointed sound, which you ignore. What happens now is up to you, not him, and you'll do with him as you see fit.

You breathe on him again, and then trail one fingernail up, from his hilt to his head, and then two finger pads, petting his cock like it's a skittish cat. His hips jerk, trying to take more contact from you, so you try to channel the dom.

"Lay down," you say, louder than you meant to, but he obeys with a startled gasp. You make your way up to his head and push a hand into his hair, clenching it lightly. The power is fun, and you immediately say what you think of next. "If you behave then I'll let you come," you say, your eyes on his. "But if you're good, then I'll make you come," you promise. His eyes go wide and he swallows.

"Yes, Mistress."

"Good." You nod, then you make your way back down to where his hips await.

You ignore the rest of him because you can, because this is the most delicious way you know to torture him. His cock is long and slender, reaching almost to his stomach, but with a wide head, and you play along it with breath, hair, hands. It writhes like a snake, stiffening up when and where you touch it, trying to match you like it knows it was meant to. Precum glistens at the end of his tip and you take your thumb to massage it over him, the lubrication matching what's gathering beneath your skirt, the wetness taking over. The head of his cock is shiny and red like an apple and the look on his face is pained as he tries not to beg you for what you know he needs.

"How badly do you want to fuck me?"

"Please," he says in a guttural voice. "Please."

You straddle him, lifting your skirt, reaching down to pull your underwear aside. You want this to be as rough and hard as possible. Reaching your hand between your legs, you take hold of his cock like you haven't yet, hear him gasp, and then set him at the entrance to your pussy. One swift slide down his shaft, and he curls up, letting out a loud moan.

"Lay down," you command again, and he goes still.

He's not the only one curling, the length of him is hard in you, and you can feel the head you were just toying with at your very back, shoved so fast and deep inside. You rise up again, playing yourself just over the head of his cock, rubbing your elastic entrance with it, tensions mounting, feeling good, until you sag down, burying him back in. He cries out, as do you, it feels so good to have him back there, throbbing in what had just been empty space before. Keeping him deep you start to grind so that your clit gets rubbed where your hips meet.

The speed and pace of everything is up to you, and you're doing what your body tells you it needs now. You pulse on top of him like he's a toy, using him, and from the way that he cries out and the increasing hardness of his cock you know he likes it. When you slow down he lets out a plaintive noise the sound of need being denied, and part of you likes your power over him.

You bend forward to take him deeper into you, and pinch one of your nipples through your shirt. Your skirt is hiding you from what you know is going on below, him saddled by your thighs, your hips hijacking his cock for their own desires, if you keep riding him like you're going, the combination of his head deep inside and your clit against his pubic bone are going to make you – make you – make you -- you scream and fuck him even harder, deeper, using the waves of your orgasm to pull him in as far as you can. You curl forward and cry out again, riding him through, using him until the very end.

You bow over him, his cock still hard and look up. On his face you can see the ferocious effort it took not to come when you did, and you can feel inside you that he's still ready, hoping for it. You brace your-self on hands and knees, looking up at him, and with a ragged voice you say, "Go."

Finally given freedom to use his knees and hips he thrusts up and in, fucking you with abandon. Your pussy is still tight around him from your orgasm and everything he's doing now still feels good, that head of his pulling you popping tight, like your pussy is a wine bottle and it's cork, in and out, in, and out, and you're surprised the friction could start to build again inside you so soon, but the wonders of his anatomy and the hotness of his condition – you send a hand down between your legs to frantically rub the slippery space around your clit, using skin and fabric both as his moans give way to grunts and he goes faster than even you were earlier, his extraordinary cock plumbing the depths of you with that head – he shouts and his hips rise up so high your knees leave the ground and leaving you pinned on top of his cock which is twitching as it releases inside of you – you scream as your second orgasm rips through you, your pussy trying to hold onto his cock again, both of you trying to stay locked together in this one moment of ecstasy until gravity and exhaustion set in.

His hips sink and you find yourself back on your knees. His cock slides out of you and you find yourself mourning its loss. You climb up the man, stroking a hand up his heaving chest.

"Mistress, have I pleased you?" he asks in a pant, expression completely earnest.

You're not breathing right yet and your heartbeat is still loud in your ears. You lean over him and kiss his lips softly, once. "Yes."

He smiles and finally relaxes. You reach behind him and pull the tie on the knot that will unlace his arms.

Before he can ask you anything else, you stand, just as unsteady as the woman that was here before, and go over to the butler, who's been waiting patiently, eyes still closed. You know he heard everything though – suit pants show erections even easier than jeans.

You assemble yourself and then tell him, "You can open your eyes now."

"As you wish," he responds and does so, giving you a reserved smile. "Shall we try another door?"

You nod.

Turn to page 76.

ou shake your head after listening. "I'm not ready for this,"
you say – and watch the butler's eyebrows rise.

"Mistress, I beg to differ. You were made for this. The
Master brought you here, didn't he?"

"Maybe he did – but who is he? How would he even know me,
much less know what's best?"

The butler spreads his elegant gloved hands. "I cannot say. And yet,
here you are, and I know he does."

You frown but it's hard to fight him – especially since you're not
ready to leave the House just yet, not while the key still swings on
your wrist and the place is still yours.

"I want to meet him," you say.

"Maybe you will. Or maybe you won't. He's a very busy man,
orchestrating all of this for you."

"But – why me?" you say.

"Mistress," the Butler says, taking your shoulders gently in his
hands. "Why not you?"

It occurs to you that the Butler must be a very patient man – and
that he probably doesn't get paid enough for all of this. You snort, and
he smiles.

"Back to the main hallway?" he asks kindly. "Or would you like to
try this fetching gray door?" he says with enough of a smile you know
it's a tease.

Back to the hallway? If so, turn to page 64.

Or back to the nearest gray door? Flip to page 77.

"Of course, Mistress," the butler says. He steps back and gestures to one side and you see a door that you hadn't seen before. "Back to the main hall," he says, and leads you there via a dimly lit passageway.

Would you like to open the purple door with men talking behind it? If so, turn to page 193.

There's still a bath being drawn behind the white door. If you'd like to visit it, turn to page 9.

The gray door still has the sound of rope rubbing over other rope. If you'd like to visit it again, turn to page 54.

And walking down the hall you see a door you hadn't seen before – its color is eggshell blue, matching the sky of the nearest painting perfectly. If you want to listen at it, turn to page 190.

"Of course, Mistress," the butler says. He steps back and the knife disappears. "We have clothing for you to change into...." He leaves the room and returns with a neatly folded stack, wearing a fresh suit of his own. Then he turns around genteelly as you change. You cough when you're through and he turns back with a bow.

"To the hall," he announces and leads you there via a dimly lit passageway.

Would you like to open the purple door with men talking behind it? If so, turn to page 193.

There's still a bath being drawn behind the white door. If you'd like to visit it, turn to page 9.

The gray door still has the sound of rope rubbing over other rope. If you'd like to visit it again, turn to page 54.

And walking down the hall you see a door you hadn't seen before – its color is eggshell blue, matching the sky of the nearest painting perfectly. If you want to listen at it, turn to page 190.

*Y*ou nod, and he nods back, agreeing with your choice.

"Of course, Mistress." He waits for you to gather yourself and stand, and then he follows suit. "Wait here."

He leaves the room and returns a few minutes later, wearing a fresh suit and holding a stack of clothing for you to change into, then turns around genteelly as you change. You cough when you're through, and he turns back with a bow.

"To the front hall," he announces, and leads you there via a dimly lit passageway.

Would you like to open the purple door with men talking behind it? If so, turn to page 193.

There's still a bath being drawn behind the white door. If you'd like to visit it, turn to page 9.

The gray door still has the sound of rope rubbing over other rope. If you'd like to visit it again, turn to page 54.

And walking down the hall you see a door you hadn't seen before – its color is eggshell blue, matching the sky of the nearest painting perfectly. If you want to listen at it, turn to page 190.

*Y*ou're nervous putting yourself into this stranger's power, but you know this is what you want. Besides, the butler is here – and you can always say red, can't you?

Before your braveness leaves you, you to turn to the dom. "Tie me," you command. He gives you a look, and it occurs to you that if this is what you want, you won't be the person giving orders anymore. "Please," you add, contrite.

He chuckles low, the sound of someone who has surprises in store, and then sobers, scaring you a little. "Turn around," he commands with a growl.

You whirl to do as you're told, surprised by how quickly your body obeys. He takes your arms and brings them behind your back roughly. "Hold your hands," he says, as he forces them together. You gasp at this, and then remember what you signed up for. But the butler's still there – your eyes lock with his and while his face is impassive, you still feel safer for his presence.

The dom leaves you where you're standing, and you feel compelled to stay still until he returns with rope. You can hear him stretch out a length and then feel him slide it up underneath your arms, the rope catching under both of your armpits at shoulder height. The rope pulls you back, momentarily giving you perfect posture as you stand straight – and then you can feel him start to twine and knot the rope down both your arms, and you realize what he's going to do – your arms will be tied behind you, leaving you helplessly dependent on him.

Your first inclination is to fight. This isn't what you wanted – is it? You open up your mouth to say something and he pauses to listen. You gave him permission to do this, you can revoke it at any time. Keeping that in mind calms you as your arms are roped up, and then you feel him lacing them tighter together behind you. You struggle, not with purpose but just to see, and find you can't get loose – there's no way you can get out of the ropes unless he sets you free.

"Kneel," he commands, and you fall to your knees. Once there, it's hard not to bend forward as if you're bowing at his feet. Then, and only then, do you hear him make a grunt of satisfaction – in you or in his handiwork, you're not sure. But you've pleased him and now that you're helpless, you find that's what you want.

Things have been magical since you entered the House, your stresses and worries have all been left behind. But this takes things to deeper level still. You realize now is when you can let everything truly go. All you are is a woman, molded by a man, meant to serve him however he wants you to. There's no thinking anymore – and as much as you'd think you'd hate it, if someone had told you of this ahead of time – in reality, utterly giving over control is bliss. Now you know why the woman strung overhead had that lost look in her eyes.

The dom kneels beside you so that he's at your bent forward level. "Do you see?" he asks, voice not unkind.

You nod. You didn't know until just now, but yes.

"Good." His knees are wide as he sits on his heels, the outline of his cock showing through his jeans. "I can let you go now. Or…" he says, without saying anything else.

Do you stay with the dom? Turn to page 70.

Do you go? Go to page 69.

"Red," you say. You could say anything, you think, but you want to say the right thing – and you want to know it works.

"As you wish," the dom says. He reaches a hand behind your back and tugs on one of the knots he's placed there. The rope spools off of your arms, and suddenly you're free. Your arms rise up of their own accord like wings, feeling free. The dom stands and bows and then leaves you alone with the butler.

"Shall we try another door?" the Butler asks.

You nod.

Turn to page 76.

ou nod your head – and what happens next surprises you. He stands, ignoring you completely. You hear rope over rope, and the sigh of the woman above you as she's released. Tilting your head you can see her draped over him, clinging, knees weak, the lines the rope has left across her making her even more beautiful than she already is. He takes her and disappears from your field of view, leaving you and the butler behind.

Even though you're not sure what will come next, the growing heat inside your hips says you want it. Do you still want the Butler here to see you though? Thinking quickly, you come up with a compromise.

"Close your eyes," you whisper to him, and he silently obeys.

The dom returns, woman gone, standing in front of you as your bound arms force you to kneel at his feet.

"What shall I do with you?" he muses, talking only to himself. He reaches down and moves your hair to look at your face, as if inspecting your mouth. Then he eyes the rest of you, gaze slightly more cold than appreciative, as if determining your worth, and somehow that's hot too, the degradation making you wet. You're just a pussy to be fucked and now that that's all you are, you find that that's all you want to be.

It's funny how being all tied up can make you leave so much behind.

The dom takes his jeans off, letting his cock fall out, hanging heavy in front of you.

"Is this what you want?" he asks, putting a hand to it, stroking himself slowly.

Yes, you want to beg, but remember yourself in time. "I only want what you want."

He smiles wickedly. "Good. Remember that." He reaches up and twines his hand through your hair and brings your mouth to the end of his cock.

He holds you there with your hair, pulling your head up so that you have to look at him. Your mouth opens of its own accord and he settles himself inside with a satisfied moan. Slowly he pulls your mouth on and off his cock, you feel it slide in and bend down where it hits the back of your throat, close to gagging on it but not quite. You're off kilter, kneeling, unable to balance with your hands, needing him to stop you from falling on your face. He groans with each of the strokes he's making you give himself, and then pulls you off of him, pushing you back onto your knees.

"Lick it," he commands, while he looks down at you. His face is impassive, as cold as his cock is hard, but he's breathing faster. You know he's pleased, even if he won't show it -- and the thought of what he might do with that cock to you is making the crotch of your underwear wet.

So you do what you're told, licking him with abandon, all along his shaft, head to hilt and back again, trying to make it so there's no part of him you haven't reached. Watching you work, he purrs, "Good." At this encouragement you try harder, you just want to see him pleased – and when he pulls his cock away from you, you let out a disappointed moan.

He chuckles. "Some women are better at this than others. I think you are one of those. Turn around."

On your knees, you do so – and hear him lowering himself behind you. Strong hands pick you up and pull you back, so that you're lying on top of his broad chest. It's awkward with your arms bound, but it doesn't last long as he rises up again, lifting you too.

"Bend your knees," he says, like his are bent.

You do as you're told, and you know he's holding you up just inches over his cock. You can feel his hand go up under your skirt to shove your panties to one side, feel him measuring the wetness there, push into your pussy, and you moan.

"You do want it, don't you," he says, his hot breath on your back.

You don't feel safe speaking, so you whine and nod.

"Say it," he says, his fingers still playing with you roughly. You're facing away from him so that all you can see is the rest of the room and the butler, eyes still closed, listening in.

"I want it," you whisper, knowing you do, still afraid you'll be denied.

But the second you say the words he pulls his hand out and settles you onto his cock in one swift slide. You gasp as he rams in, no pretense of foreplay – but you didn't need any, you're already so wet. Behind you, he's holding onto the binding of your arms like reins with one hand, the other hand is braced behind him, so he can maximize his thrusts. You try to move but can't – with your arms tied, there's no where you can go, which you realize was his plan. He wanted to keep you still so that he could fuck you just like he needs to fuck.

The dom likes things fast. He's pounding into you, opening you up, and you cry out – after all that time licking his cock, it feels just as good inside of you as you thought it would – and the violence of his thrusts turns your cry into a waver. The sound of you makes him even faster, harder, and he leans forward a little still pulling you back onto him, so that you're trapped on his cock.

"Do you like that?" he asks you, not caring what your answer is. He raises up his other hand and slaps you across your ass, and you cry out anew. "Do you?"

"Yes," you hiss as he fucks you so fast. The slap was something new and strange and it changed everything. He changes hands on the arm-binding reins and slaps your ass from the other side, the sound crisp in the room.

He lets go of your arms and grabs hold of your hips and starts ramming you down on top of his cock. You've never been taken this roughly before, or maybe you have, but you've never felt quite this used. You can't believe how much it turns you on, when all you can do is hold on for the ride. Every time his cock pulls in and out it tugs your underwear beside it, and your underwear strokes your clit and it's good but it's not good enough and you whine in need.

"Do you want to come, girl?" he asks.

"Yes," you hiss, your voice rising as you say it.

With a pull and a tug, rope spills from your arms and they're suddenly free. It feels like you've been given wings, they feel lighter than air, as he pushes himself forward and up, still in you as you drop to all fours. He grabs hold of your hair and pulls your head back, keeping you pinned on his cock, and growls. "Rub yourself for me."

You lunge your hand between your thighs, finding your clit there as his cock pulses in and out. You press three fingers in and stroke yourself wide and fast and your hips start to work with his, sharing in his hunger.

"Ask for permission," he growls from above.

You want to say, permission for what? But you know what he wants – not just to fuck you but to own you fully. You rub yourself hard, his cock thudding in and out, balls slapping at your hand with each of his strokes, you get yourself just to the edge, where you're about to take off, just like your arms wanted to fly before – "Please," you ask, with a quiver in your voice.

"Please what?" he asks, without slowing down, making it hard for you to wait.

"Please, can I come -- please."

He takes his hands and spreads your ass cheeks wide so that he can fuck even deeper parts of you, and starts to go more slowly. "How bad do you need it?"

"So bad," you say, hoping it's not a trick question. "Oh God, so bad."

"Are you sure?" His cock is rock hard inside you, and arrow straight, you know that he's got to be close too, but he still finds time to torture you with each slow stroke, and you're afraid to touch your clit anymore because you might set yourself off, but your underwear are still being pushed and pulled against your clit as he moves and there's a chance that will bring you off too --

"I need it so bad," you say, your voice rising in desperation. "I've got to come. Please, please, please –" you start begging, breathless with each hotter stroke.

He settles himself deep inside you again. "Then come for me," he growls, and starts fucking you even faster than before. You feel the head of him at the back of you and his cock is so hard and you know if you go he'll go too and so you work your clit and then – your orgasm suffuses every part of you as you cry out, your pussy clenching tight around his cock, trying to make him fill it up – and he does, frantically fucking your pussy like it was meant to be fucked, using the last of your orgasm to pull out his.

He shouts out and follows you through, the friction of him inside of you making your orgasm last even longer, and he takes forever to slow down, enjoying the last of the heat between the two of you.

He lets you go and you fall forward, suddenly earthbound, and he catches you quickly and takes you back on his lap. "Are you okay?"

You nod, still lost for words. His eyes search yours – the demeanor before was all for show. Despite treating you like you were trash, he knows you're not, and he knows that a woman that will let him fuck them like that is a rare creature indeed.

"Are you sure?" he says, with half a smile, brushing hair out of your face, watching you carefully.

"It's just strange is all."

"As long as strange is good," he says, now smiling fully. He stands and takes you up with him, and this is part of it too, you feel, him making sure you land normally after soaring so high on endorphins.

"Is it always like that?" you ask him, leaning into his chest, letting him hold you up.

"If you do it right." He carefully straightens your shirt and skirt for you, even reaching up to pull your underwear down to where they normally rest on your hips. The room smells like sex and there's a river between your legs, but somehow the spinning is slowing down and things are going back to normal. His hands on you now are gentle – not the same hands that were yanking your arms back, or your hair, or slapping at your ass. You realize that for as hard as he was fucking you, he was always in control, even of himself. He could have not fucked you at all – or he could have denied you your orgasm.

"Thank you," you say.

He takes up your hand and kisses it, like an old-time courtier. "No, thank you. Not many doms will tell you, but the sub is always the one really in control."

It didn't feel like that – because you didn't want it too. Without your willingness to be dominated, a dom would have no fun. You smile at him and take your hand back, and step away, feeling reality return. It's the same, but you know that you've changed.

You turn and walk over to the Butler. His eyes are still closed, but suit-pants show erections even better than jeans.

"You may open your eyes now."

"Yes, Mistress." His dark brown eyes take you in, and he breathes deep, and you wonder if he likes what he smells. "Would you like to open another door?"

"Yes, please," you say. He takes your elbow, and directs you to the back of the room.

Turn to page 76.

he door at the back of the room set up for ropes is cold gray stone and crossed wooden beams, lashed together with pieces of black leather. Pressing your ear to it you hear the report of a whip like a gunshot, quickly followed by a man's guttural groan.

If you want to go inside turn to 77.

Would you like to go back to the hallway? If so, turn to 63.

ou swing the key up on your bracelet and use it to open up the gray door's lock. It opens and you step inside.

This room is larger than the last, although the décors the same, sumptuous fabrics, couches, rugs, and candlelight – but in the center of this room a wooden X stands, propped up like an artist's easel, with an empty X on the opposite side.

A blindfolded man is chained on this, his back to you, fastenings at his wrists and ankles, and a woman holding a whip is standing beside him. She's trailing her hand down his back, inspecting her recent handiwork. Red stripes crisscross him, and he's completely naked while she's clothed, wearing a sheath dress of black latex, which barely covers her breasts or comes down her thighs.

She looks over her shoulder and spots you and the butler, and gives both of you curt nods. You may be the House's Mistress, but you're in her domain now.

She stalks over and gives you an almost military bow. "Greetings, Mistress. What would you like to know?"

There's a stand beside the sub she's whipping, and it holds all sorts of things you've never seen. There are whips that end in strands of fur, whips that look like riding crops, whips that have many ends, and whips that have just one, tipped with steel.

"What were you doing to him just now?" you ask her.

She smiles. "Warming him up. Would you like to help?"

"I – I don't want to hurt him."

The domme smiles even wider. "Why not? That's rather the point. If you mean you don't want to do anything wrong though – I can help with that."

"I want to see first. Can you keep going?"

"Of course," she says, and returns to her weapons rack. She picks up two multi-tendrilled floggers and starts in on him, working hand over hand, creating a continual sweeping pattern on his back, the landing of the leather strips sounding like rain.

You walk around to the other side. He doesn't look like he's hurting. From here, he looks like he's being attacked by one of the rollers in a mechanical car wash. You lean in and push his blindfold up. "Do you like it?"

"No," he says, giving you pause. "I like it when it hurts more."

The domme chuckles. "Don't think I didn't hear you."

She walks around to your side of the cross and puts a whip handle in his mouth like a bit. "Talk again and I'll use that on you."

"I wouldn't dream of it," he says, letting the whip fall to the floor. She snatches it up and cracks it across his ass, hard, and you wince as his fists clench and he goes up on his toes. But he rides the pain through just like you've ridden a cock and when he gasps aloud he sounds satisfied.

She holds the whip she was using up, it has one single whip-tail and it's short. "Never the kidneys, and never anywhere too soft on him – and never anywhere too hard," she says, swinging to indicate that hardness would be her fault. "But you can strike a person's back, buttocks, breasts, and thighs fairly safely if you practice and you start slow. Would you like to help me dominate him? Or would you like to join him?" She gestures at the open space with a sly smile. "I've got an empty side."

Do you want to help her dominate him? Turn to 79.

Do you want to be whipped too? Turn to 85.

ou look at the unblindfolded man – and his expression says, *Try me.*

"I'd like to learn," you say.

"Good choice," the domme agrees. You cast one glance over at the watchful butler, and then join her on her side. She jerks her chin at you and then tells you to turn around and lift up your shirt.

You hesitate, frowning.

"You can't know what it's like to hit another person until you've been hit yourself, first."

It makes a certain sense – and the butler is still here. You angle yourself away from him and her and lift your shirt up to your neck.

"You need to know what it's like but trust me, I won't hit you hard." She reaches forward and moves your hair out of the way, and then you feel the weight of the floggers land on you. They're the same ones she was just using on the man and they don't hurt – it's rather like getting a massage. They brush over your shoulder blades and down, and then she lashes them up the backs of your thighs, to land gently on skin otherwise hidden by your skirt. "But too close – or too hard –" she says, demonstrating, and the flogger tails land on you all at once, twenty at a time, not with sharp pain, but all of them at once feel like she's hit you with a wall -- you stagger forward as she says, "Practice and careful observation are key."

The domme stops, lesson finished, and you pull your shirt back down. When you turn she's standing, offering the same flogger out to you.

You take it. It's almost the length of your arm, the handle the size and width of a generous cock, ending in twenty different black leather tassels.

"Start from here," the domme says, measuring your swing space with a critical eye. "Start slow. Aim high."

The man on the cross ducks his face down between the top V, which you're glad for, if you hit him there this experiment would be over. You take an overhead swing at him, too gently, the tassels fall before they reach him. The domme watches you, with one eyebrow quirked. You concentrate harder, and go again.

This time they land. They snap against his right shoulder before sliding down his back, whip heavy in your hand. You bring the whip up again, and aim for the other shoulder, this time, a little harder – and leave red welts on his back. The man tied up on the cross moans.

You've never whipped another person before, but you can see how it would be enjoyable. He's helpless and utterly exposed, trusting you to both hurt him but also make him feel good, aiming for that space where pain and goodness overlap to blossom like a strange and exotic flower. You hit him again, and again, you're not as fast as the domme was, and you've only got one whip going, but each time you land a blow he shivers.

The domme leans in to whisper. "Change it up."

Bolder now, you aim for his ass, whisking it with the whip. He jumps and then moans and you strike first one thigh, then the other, the red welts you're creating beginning to cover him, like you're painting a picture of pain on his back.

The domme holds up her hand for you to stop and you do so. Then she walks over to him, and strokes him like a pet.

"Ready for more?" she asks him solicitously. You see the man nod. When she returns to you, she grabs another tool off her rack to hand to you.

This one has shorter tassels and the leather's stiffer too. The domme adjusts your stance and nods.

You start up slow again. This time he cries out when blows land – but he doesn't say red to stop you. His hands clench and he goes up on his toes and you've never been in control of a man quite like this. You're giving him what he wants by hurting him – and hurting him because he wants it is turning you on.

You work on both his shoulders, and then surprise him by lashing his ass, making his hips jerk sideways in surprise. You strike his thighs, then his back again, making the whip dance over him with stinging blows. He grunts and groans like he's fucking the cross or being fucked but he doesn't tell you to stop.

The domme's the one who puts her hand out to stop you. "He's done for, I can tell."

You look from him to her and back again. "But he hasn't told me."

"No, but it's our job to be discerning," she says. "Those who give can give too much."

You follow her to the rack, where you can see what you've done to the man chained there clearly. His back is covered in rising red – you know the next time he showers or puts a shirt on, it will burn.

"I did that," you say, half-a-question, half-a-claim.

"You did," the domme agrees. She offers him water, which he sips. It seems odd to see her being kind to someone she just whipped, but she sees the look in your eyes before you can ask. "Just because I have control of things doesn't mean I want to break them. Part of being a domme is taking care of your property."

The key that names you Mistress of this House swings against your wrist. "Then shouldn't I be the one to care for him?"

The domme's lips purse. You do out rank her. "If you wish, Mistress."

Turn to 82.

"I'll do it," you demand. You're the one who hurt him after all. The domme nods and gives the water to you.

"There's a bathroom over there," she says, pointing towards one corner of the room. "Help him wash." Then she leaves.

"Are you okay?" you ask the sub. He nods, and you look at all his chains. Luckily you have a key – and it works on his nearest wrist lock.

Unlocking everything gives you the chance to see what you've done up close. The welts are like a map over his body, angry, red. You make a pained sound on his behalf, unlocking his last ankle, and he shakes his head.

"Don't apologize." He's still panting a little from the pain, his expression distant, drugged on his own endorphins. He's clinging to the cross to stand.

"Let me help you," you suggest, and take his nearest hand.

He staggers into you, drapes an arm around your neck, and you make your way into the bathroom together, leaving the butler alone outside.

This bathroom is small for convenience's sake. There's just a shower and a toilet, no tub – and of course all of the towels in the bathroom are white. You take one off the wall and offer it to him, and he shakes his head. "I want to shower. And then I probably want ibuprofen."

He smiles at you, and you smile back. He's trying to make you feel better about having hurt him, which you realize shouldn't actually be his job. Even if you're not the domme, you are the Mistress.

"Stand here," you command him, and sensing the change in your voice, he does, stock still.

You lean into the shower and start the water running. When you find a medium temperature, neither too cold or too hot, nothing that would make his welts sting, you tell him to get in.

He does so then looks at you, eyes hot, waiting for the next command to obey.

You reach in and grab the soap and unwrap it, and take a white washcloth off of the stack by the door. Then you soap it and look at him again. "Show me your back."

He turns, and braces himself against the far wall of the shower, as you reach through the curtain of water and set the washcloth against his shoulder.

He hisses and cries out, contact and soap making fresh welts burn. You lift the washcloth, and tamp it down a few inches over, and he rises up on his toes.

"I have to clean you off," you say, apology and explanation.

"I know," he gasps, as you do so.

You make your way down his back, then over the curve of his ass, and squat to wash off his thighs, taking care of all the places you were responsible for damaging.

"Turn around. Rinse off," you command him, and he does. He winces and closes his eyes as his back takes the full brunt of the shower spray, lashing him anew where you just cleaned.

You take a fresh washcloth and hand the bar of soap over to him. "Bathe," you command, sitting down to watch him on the closed toilet.

He takes the soap and washcloth from you and lathers it up. Then, eyes on you, he starts washing himself. He has hair on his chest and under his arms and over his cock, and the water makes it lie in dark patterns against him. He's been naked this whole time but watching him wash himself, trapped in this small bathroom together, makes him seem somehow more exposed, and you know he feels it too.

His hands start high, washing his face, wetting his hair, and then sink lower, soaping under armpits and down arms, and then slowly down his stomach, hands reaching for his cock. It's semi-hard but his mouth opens as he touches it, and he looks at you for permission.

It's your job to take care of him, isn't it?

"Keep going," you say, and he groans, continuing to stroke himself, soap rinsing away from him so that you can see his growing hard-on as he works. He pulls his hand up to the end of himself, strokes his tip, and then plunges back down. You can tell he's using a rhythm that he's used solo before, he's working himself like a pro, watching you, then watching himself, his free hand bracing him on the shower door, water still pouring down. From the noises he's making and the concentration on his face, you know he's getting close. You stand, and he stops.

"Did I tell you to stop?" you ask him, voice stern.

He shakes his head fast.

"Then keep going," you say, leaning in. You practically step into the shower with him, standing right in front of his naked body, and reach around him. "I like watching you fuck yourself," you whisper into his ear.

He makes a strangled sound at this, his hand almost touching your stomach each stoke, as your hand finds the temperature control knob at the back. You wait until he's ready to cry out, stroking himself so hard and so fast you know he can't help but come – and then you flip the hot water back on.

The water hits his wounds the moment of his orgasm. He arcs forward with the force of his load coming, and then stinging water lands and he shouts out again in pain. Pain and pleasure mix in him, sensations stretching his orgasm out, and he shouts until his voice goes hoarse, then sags to kneel inside the shower at your feet. You reach in and turn the water off, and watch him pant on the ground, steam rising around you both.

"Thank you, Mistress," he manages to get out.

You hand him a towel. "You're very welcome. Will you be all right alone?"

He looks up at you, smiling and content. "Oh yes."

You smile back and reach for the door, taking an extra towel for yourself, and walk back outside.

"Mistress," the butler says, acknowledging you as you near.

"Is there another door?" you ask him.

"Always," he says, and leads the way.

Turn to 90.

ou look at the man, who obviously likes being hit, and at the domme, who seems the soul of professionalism – and the butler, your guard, standing near.

"Why not?" you say, feeling bold. She smiles wickedly at you.

"Why not indeed? Take off your shirt and bra and skirt."

Her tone is demanding – but you asked for it. You take your clothing off, like she said, leaving only your underwear on, hiding your breasts from the butler with your arms.

"Come here," she says and points to the cross. You stand in front of it, and she locks your ankles into shackles, snug, but not too tight. Then she reaches for your arm, and you realize just what you've gotten yourself into here. One wrist, and then the other, and then it's too late, as she moves your hair off to one side. There's a gap between you and the wood, but not much of one, there's no way you could get free. Across from you, you can see the other sub, and he can see you. Your breasts are pressed up against the cross's wood.

"Head down. Here it comes," he whispers at you, a moment before her first blow lands.

Whatever she's hit you with has multiple tassels, they land against your right shoulder in a strange pattern and then drag down. She hits your shoulder again, and then the other one, and it feels almost like you're getting a massage given to you by cat-paws. She brushes this whip over your back, then surprises you when you feel it against your ass, and stroking up your thighs. She flicks the whip between your legs, letting it land against your crotch with weight but no sting, but you still jump in surprise.

Then she moves away from you and over to him. He groans as whatever she's using hits him, biting his lips in pain. You can hear it land over different parts of him, watch him wince, hear him moan, feel the cross shake as his body tries to get away. But he doesn't say red or tell her to stop – if he can be that strong, so can you, you decide.

Your turns comes up. The whip has sharper leather now, and it cracks when it hits your flesh, and you gasp. You're not as stoic as the man was, and the whip hurts, but it doesn't hurt for long, it's like a sting and then it fades, leaving only the memory of pain. She starts slowly across your shoulders, down your back, slapping at then striking your ass with it as you jerk from side to side, trying to escape. Then another dull thud across your crotch as you cry out in surprise – only to realize she's used the more gentle whip again. She chuckles as you sag against your chains, heart racing from the fear of pain – and find your pussy getting wet at the thought of more.

She leaves you there hanging, literally, and goes back to the other sub. He cries out at the force of her blows, the whip she's using on him singing through the air before it cracks against his skin, and after each strike he moans. When she moves to you again, you're frightened and turned on in equal measure, even though you can't precisely explain why. You know you're going to be hurt and you're going to like it and parts of you deep inside are beginning to ache.

The whip lands on your ass with a crack and you shake and shout. She swings the duller whip between your legs again, making you go up on your toes in surprise, feeling the leather cup and curve against your crotch, tickling your thighs – and then the sharper whip strikes your other ass-cheek. The domme hits you twice between your legs now, and between the pain and the longing and the not knowing what's coming next, you moan.

"How much more do you think you can take?" she asks you, as she slaps lower, stinging the back of one whole thigh.

You want to say you can take the world, because you think you can, but you're not thinking straight – "More –" you gasp out.

Another stroke between your legs and cat-paw-leather pressing everywhere, and then another slap on your thigh.

"More," you beg, and she hits both places again. Pleasure from the pressure, the straps of leather on your upper thighs and underwear-protected clit, and then the pain of the snap – "More –"

She makes a considering noise, and stops. "No."

"But –" you lift your head to look back at her. You're the mistress of the house, even though you're chained.

She places a hand on your back and runs it down your ass to your thigh. A track of fire follows her touch and you moan.

"Your skin's not used to this. Though it could be, given time." She leans in to look at both of you. You're panting, a river of need flowing between your legs, and the other sub is still breathing hard. She unlocks your ankles and then your wrists, and you fall into her. She catches you, stronger than you are, and steadies you on your feet.

"Are you okay?" For someone who was just whipping you, she seems authentically concerned.

"I am. I'm just –" There's no way to explain to her how you feel right now. Elated, scared, sore, turned on.

"I know." She starts walking with you to the side of the room. "Let's get you clean before you move on," she says, and takes you into a small bathroom after collecting all your clothing.

"See?" she says, once you're inside. You look over your shoulder at yourself in the mirror and see your own back streaked with red. There is beauty in it, like the domme has given you a tiger's stripes.

She then sets you on the closed toilet, limp as a rag doll, and turns on the water in the shower, pulling you to standing to take off your panties before guiding you inside. The water feels heavy where it hits, not unlike the whip, and you reach out for the shower wall and moan. Standing there it's easy to get lost again, steam rising up, water pouring down – until the domme starts dabbing washcloths at your back.

You hiss in surprise and pain and sink down. She follows you, and even though her hand is light she's making your back sing.

"It hurts," you say.

"I know," she agrees. She reaches up and takes the showerhead attachment down. "Turn around," she commands, and you do so. "Stand still," she demands, and you do that, too.

She's holding the shower head like a whip, and she uses it just the same, only this time on the front of you. Your breasts are lashed with water, first hot, then cold, then hot again. She twists the nozzle and turns the spray into a jet, bringing it inches from your skin, letting the water pummel you. Your back stings when it's against the cold tile wall of the shower, and it stings when it's not, and steam's rising all around. Water is beading on the domme's short latex dress – things are spinning again, when you realize that she's purposefully moving the water, over your stomach and up your thighs, until she abandons pretense and sets the shower nozzle beneath your clit.

It's like a thousand tongues lapping up – until she changes the settings and it's a hot jet – and then stinging rain, like the whip she used on you before. You can't get used to any of her changes, but it doesn't matter, soon everything is feeling good, hot, cold, sharp, soft. Your hips start rocking off of the wall, and the domme growls until they're still again – she's in control of you, not you, no matter how much you need.

She starts to shake her hand between your legs now, making the spray quiver, so that it presses up between your labia and underneath your hood, making your clit dance. You make noises you haven't heard before, small cries of submission, rising up on your toes, chained to the wall behind you without chains as she brings the water in.

"Should I let you come?" she asks, moving the water briefly away.

"Yes. Please, yes," you beg.

"Because it would make you happy?" she says, a question. You look up at her and see her as turned on as you are by the control she has over you now, even more than when she was holding a whip.

"Because it would make you happy," you say, a statement. Her lips quirk up, she laughs, and she moves the nozzle back into place, leaning over you, moving her hand back and forth, making the spray of water shake like you know that you're about to when you come. You're so close and the water won't stop and neither will she -- you cry out and your orgasm flows over you like the water does, hot and wet. She purrs, still in control as you writhe in front of her, pinned to the wall by the water and her presence, even though your knees feel weak.

She steps back and you stagger and catch yourself, taking in huge gulps of steaming air. She offers you a towel – and you use it to blot off her dress, before using it on yourself. You can tell by the way she watches you she approves.

Then she reaches for the door.

"But –" you protest as she opens it, letting in cooler air.

She reaches back to touch your cheek and smile fondly. "You're not my only sub," she says, and goes, leaving you to collect your panties off the floor.

Putting on your bra hurts, as does the act of wearing your shirt. But you pull yourself together and leave the bathroom. The X is empty, the domme and other sub have gone elsewhere for their after-care. Only your butler still remains, standing very near the door.

"If you had called I would have heard you," he says, apologizing for not following you inside.

"It's okay. The room wasn't large enough for three." Although standing so near he must have heard everything else said and done inside. You would feel ashamed, but he's been calm and understanding so far.

"Are you ready for another door, Mistress?"

If you are, turn to 90.

ou nod, pushing back a lock of wet hair. The butler leads you to a door at the back of the whip room, so gray it's almost black.

"This door and the next are not for everyone," the butler warns you quietly. "And the only way out of it is to go through, I'm afraid. Unless you'd like to go back."

"Can you tell me anything about it?" you ask him, and he shakes his head.

"To warn you would be to ruin it. Fear is part of its allure – although remember, you can always say red."

Do you go back to the hallway? If so, go to page 64.

If you choose to continue, forewarned, turn to 91.

ou chew a little on your lower lip. You've already been brave this far, haven't you? What's one more door – especially when the butler's still at your side?

"I'm glad I have you here," you say, honest.

"I'm glad to be here, Mistress," he says with a nod.

You take his gloved hand in your free one and use your other to open the lock.

The door swings open to reveal a room that's half-laboratory, half-church. Back-lit stained glass lines the walls, showing kaleidoscopic fractals, lighting up what looks like an altar lined with candles, an array of implements, and a strange purple-glowing thing.

As you take another step in, a person resolves from the dark, almost impossible to see because they're dressed in black – and wearing an all-black mask. You gasp and lean into the butler.

"He may be frightening, but he's a master at his work," the butler murmurs under his breath.

You swallow and nod, taking a tentative step forward. The masked man gestures to the table – which you gather he wants you to lay down on.

You hop onto it and curl into a ball, knees to chin. He reaches for your shirt, to pull it off of you and you give it to him, then he reaches for your underwear and bra. You take these off more reluctantly, folding them to keep them nearby.

His hands tap at the bottom of the table, where there are chains, and you know what he wants next. You give him one ankle and watch him latch it, and then the other too. The tools surrounding him didn't get any less frightening for you being chained nearby. He moves to the head of the table and taps for your attention – and wrists.

"I –" you protest, unsure.

The butler comes up, ready to rescue you, and you get an idea.

"What if you just hold me down instead?"

"You can always say red, Mistress," he reminds you.

You look from the masked man to the tools, some of them with points. "Please."

"All right then." The butler takes a place at the head of the table, and you lay down, heart pounding hard. You stretch your arms up over your head and he takes one wrist in each hand, pressing down. When you look up and back you can see him there, brow furrowed, face intent, sharp features drawn sharper by concern. You've been so busy on your own journey that you haven't realized that he's beautiful –

Something warm and hot hits the top of your foot. You gasp aloud and look down. The man with a mask is holding a candle up over you, letting wax drop down, and now he has all your attention.

Wax can go places whips can't. You watch him circle the table, raise the candle again, and know that your belly's going to get burned – wax falls, shimmering in the candle light, spattering to land across your belly like spent cum. Each drop lands hot then cools, marking you.

The higher the candle, the cooler the wax – the closer, the more that it burns you. He takes another candle up and waves them like he's conducting an orchestra over you, sending drizzles of white wax down. You never know where it will land next, or how hot it will be, and the not knowing and the pain and the release of when it cools sets you writhing. Chains rattle against your feet, but the butler's hands keep your hands still – you open closed eyes to see the butler watching you intently for an instant before he looks away like he's been caught.

The play of wax stops – the masked man puts on gloves covered in soft fur and strokes you down, head to toe, like you're a cat getting pet with cat fur. He wraps his fingers around every part of you, his thoroughness almost clinical, as he strokes up between your thighs, and over both your breasts, up your neck, brushing against your ear, your face, the palms of your hands, the bottoms of your feet. You shiver with goosebumps and you hear the butler's breath hitch, although the masked man himself is completely unresponsive. As good as this feels, you get the feeling it's an interlude and wonder what he has planned next.

He moves to stand at the bottom of the table where you can see, and takes off the soft gloves, then reaches for another set to pull on. These look like black leather until he turns them towards you, palms out, and you can see they're lined with spikes.

You gasp, barely having time to be frightened, before he sets one palm down on your leg. The sensation is strange, like pinpricks, but gentle. He clasps his hands on you, never pushing that hard down, but moving slowly up both of your legs. Pinpricks follow pinpricks – and then the lightest of scratchings as he pulls his hands back down.

You moan at this. It sometimes feels so good to get scratched – and to have someone else scratch you all over feels divine.

He reaches your thighs, and then moves to the side of the table, bending over, and makes a gesture over you that indicates he wants you to let them spread. Nervous, but still bold, you let your legs slide open, and his spike-covered gloves move in. He clasps you more, hands moving higher, reaching fingers for the more delicate flesh inside your thighs. The pinpricks are scarier now, even though nothing about them has changed, other than their proximity to your other more private flesh.

Then he abandons your legs and moves up to your arms, leaning over you to do so. He clasps and pulls and clasps and pulls and nerves that've spent their whole lives quiet wake up. He works his way towards your armpits and you instinctively fight to cover them up, but the butler holds you back. You look up at him like he's betrayed you, and see him watching the other man, judging for himself how much he thinks you can take. You relax under his protection, and stifle a squeal when the spiked gloves reach the sensitive skin inside your upper arm.

The man skips your armpits, and begins working on the rest of you, fluttering his hands, pin sensations landing, scratching, lifting, and then landing again. He follows the line of your neck down, covering the front of your throat, places a palm between your breasts, and then another hand on your stomach, needling you there. You tense your arms, but the butler's there, still holding them back. You feel safer instantly, even though he's the one helping hold you down.

The masked man cups your breasts open handedly, avoiding your nipples, holding each in one spiked palm, picking them up so that gravity makes the pinpricks set in, not him. Then he leans over you, inspecting you with eyes hidden by his mask, and you know what he's going to do next an instant before he does it – he reaches for your nipples.

You cry out in honest fear, arching up, and then are afraid to pull away. He's holding your nipples between spiked thumb and forefinger and it feels good but it could so easily feel awful if he did the wrong thing. He pinches fractionally harder, and then lets go, and takes fresh aim, moving so his next touch finds different nerves to spike. You cry out again, this time though because it feels good, it shouldn't, but it does. He moves to take your breast fully in one hand and massage it with the spikes, reaching his other down between your thighs again, and you open without him asking this time, letting him play his hand up finger by finger like he's scaling a piano, needles getting closer and closer to your hottest spot – you spread your legs wide and he reaches in for your labia like he's reaching to pluck a flower. He holds them together, spikes sending shivers up nerves on both sides, and then spreads them apart with his finger, to hold one, then the other, pins where they were never meant to be, and yet somehow making you feel alive.

Your body is tense on his table, back arched, breasts high, hips drawn back, knees wide, your mouth open. He plays with your nipple again and you gasp, afraid and yet hopeful about what will come next, when he withdraws. You sag back down, feeling empty – and realizing that you're desperately turned on.

The gloves come off, and new plain ones take their place, he takes the time to show you – before picking up the glowing thing you saw before. It crackles with purple neon inside, and you wonder what it could be, when he takes up something else that looks like a whip only shorter, with lashes of foil instead of leather. He brings this down on your hip and it showers you with flickers of sharp pain and sparks – electricity.

He whisks down your thighs and up your stomach, leaving a colorful trail of lightning and pain, and you writhe away from the wand but towards him. He whisks the bottoms of your feet as you whimper, and then snaps it up between your thighs, and you cry aloud.

"Mistress?" the butler asks you, concerned.

You shake your head, breathing deeply in. "I'm fine."

The masked man takes that as a challenge you fear, whipping at your stomach and breasts, your tender inner arms, your thighs, your throat, always snapping back between your legs, sending jolts of literal electricity through you, equaling the best pain and worst pleasure you've ever felt. You close your eyes and want to know when this will end at the same time you don't want it to ever stop, and you hear him turn up a dial, and the pain is redoubled when he begins again. You cry out and the butler says, "Stop."

The masked man does so.

Your eyes flutter open. Trails of electricity feel like they're still soaring through you, creating new pathways, just like nerves or veins. You're breathing heavy and fast and you feel dizzy and light. Despite being chained and held on the table, it doesn't feel like any part of you is really on the ground.

The masked man changes gloves again, back to the furred ones from before. He starts massaging life back into you with these, starting lightly, then going harder, until you want to purr. A hand slides between your legs and your hips rock towards him, but then he takes his hand away.

You hear and feel the chains on your feet release just as it feels like you land. You look around at the room, which is a hundred times less frightening now, at the butler and the man.

"But –" you say, your question hanging in the air.

The butler offers you a hand to help you off the table. "He's done."

"Really?" You weren't sure you could take more, but you might have been willing to try.

The butler gives you a sly smile. "That's all there is in this room, I'm afraid."

This is the first time you haven't been sated in the entire house.

You've needed to come and been denied before, of course, but after a string of satisfaction this one night, being denied here feels wrong.

"Are you sure?" you ask.

The butler nods. "I am." He stands to one side, politely looking away as you pull your clothes back on, and when you clear your throat again he turns. From your position near the table, you can see an ominously black door, and you take a step towards it.

"Remember what I said. This next door is not for everyone," he reminds you. "Do you still want to go in?"

If you choose to exit, turn to 64.

If you choose to enter, turn to page 97.

"I'm not everyone," you remind him.

His lips lift in a subtle smile. "Of course, Mistress."

You straighten your shoulders and pull out your key.

FITTINGLY, the black door opens into a largely black room. You step inside, and the butler follows.

"What, the Master of the house couldn't pay his candle bill in here?" you say, and the butler snorts, as the door closes solidly behind him.

You look around the room. There is furniture in it, tables, couches, books, but everything's as dark as the room is, and only lit via indirect light. There's no other person there, no tools, no table – you were half-expecting a medieval torture rack. You turn back towards the butler, who's leaning against the closed door, taking off both of his gloves. "I don't get it," you say, shaking your head.

"You know how I said the only way through the last room was through the masked man?" he says, and you nod. There's something in his eyes now that frightens you a little, as he sets his gloves aside. He nods at your realization, standing tall again. "Mistress, the only way out of this room is through me."

"What do you mean?" you say, backing up. Your hip hits a table, sending it rattling.

He moves his wrist and a knife drops out of his coat and into his gloved hand. "You already know." He takes a step towards you. "Say red at any time and this is over. Or don't and –"

The way he's breathing and the way he's looking at you – and the way he's holding a knife now – you're scared yet inexplicably turned on. Desire and dread fall into your hips like twin lead weights.

The butler waits one long moment, eyeing you, giving you a chance to decide.

Do you say red to leave the room? If so, flip to page 99.

Or are you staying? Turn to 100.

"*R*ed –" you say, quickly.

The butler nods as though he expected this, and he turns around to set the knife down on the bookcase that's beside him. His demeanor changes, he's less threatening now by a factor of ten. Then he looks at you expectantly.

"Now…what?" you ask him.

"I will take you back to the main hall. The choices there are yours, as they always have been."

"Really?" you ask, voice high, heart still lodged somewhere in your throat.

Turn to 64.

$\mathcal{H}$e advances on you and you back up as he does so, finding yourself trapped against the back of a couch. Now there's no place you can run that he can't reach you. He grabs your shirt and uses it to pull you close, making you gasp.

He takes the fabric that he holds and cuts it off, throwing a piece of it to the ground. Then he grabs your collar and slices through that, and shoves the remains of your shirt roughly down. He pulls your bra straps out and cuts through them, one by one, so that your whole chest is exposed. Then he leans in and sets the knife – which you now know is sharp – to your throat.

"Tell me you want me to fuck you – or say red."

Inside his suit his cock is rock hard against your thigh, and you're spinning again like you were just before, endorphins and breathing too much air.

He grabs your hand with his free hand and puts it on his cock, and then sets the flat of the knife against your neck where you can feel its cool promise.

"Tell me."

Sanity says say red, but sanity isn't paying attention to the outline of his cock, and how hard it feels under your hand or the feelings stirring inside your hips.

Say red? Turn to 101.

Or stay and get fucked? Turn to page 103.

anity does mind the knife, though. "Red, red –" you say, lifting up on your toes to get away from it.

He lets it fall, instantly. "I'm sorry, Mistress – " he says and steps back, giving you space. You cling to the back of the couch for a long moment, completely disheveled by him. He seems like a different person when you next look up, back to being more safe and trustworthy again. The knife is gone, presumably hidden in one of his suit pockets.

"Do people really like that?" you ask him. He nods.

"Certainly. It's hard to say who though, ahead of time. The House tries to please everyone, but it is possible to go too far." He presses a hand to his chest as though personally dismayed for upsetting you, and half-bows. "We have more clothing for you – and I can take you to the first hall again, if you would like."

You swallow, calming down, your racing heart slowing. Returning sounds good. But you can figure out what you want next in a second – right now, you want to understand what happens here. "Why would anyone choose this?"

The corners of his lips lift up, letting a shadow of the man he just was shine through. "Some people like to give away control. Some people like having control taken from them. What people find desirable is complicated, sometimes even to the people themselves."

You look around the room. It's dim, but plain – not like the other rooms that got you here with their dungeon-like set-pieces.

It occurs to you that the only set piece in here is him. Your eyes search his and his gaze is steady, unafraid to let you look for answers.

"What would have happened…if I had stayed?"

His smile becomes infinitely more wicked. "Telling you isn't the same as showing you, Mistress. But if you'd like to find out, I would still be happy to oblige."

You bite your lips, considering – and your heart begins to race again as he takes a step towards you, pulling the knife out again. He advances, pressing his knee in between your legs, setting the knife against your throat just where it had been, using his other hand to take one of yours and settle it back against his still hard cock. Then he leans forward, almost setting his forehead against yours.

"It's not too late to tell me you want to get fucked," he says, voice low.

Do you choose to go back to the first set of doors? If so, flip back to 65.

If you want him to continue, go to 103.

*D*espite your fear and the wisdom of sanity, you press your hand hard against his cock. "I want to get fucked," you say, swallowing hard. He growls at this, and three things happen all at once. He pulls the knife back, spins you around, and shoves your skirt high. You're facing the front of the couch now and he bends you over it without invitation and slaps your ass, hard. You squeal in surprise, feel him pull your underwear out of your crotch and push them aside.

There's a second of delay where he's unzipping himself and you feel as alive as you feel ashamed, your ass up in the middle of a room with a stranger, your own juices staining the back of someone else's couch – then he's free of his pants and he's shoving himself into you. He doesn't ask, he just takes, and it's good because you want to be taken. He pushes you forward so that you're all hips and ass and he fucks you into the back of the couch, your thighs smashed helplessly. You try to balance on the pillows with your arms and he shoves you down, he doesn't want you doing anything, you're just the pussy that he wants to fuck.

He grabs hold of your hips and your feet are off the ground and he's thrusting into you like a jack hammer. Your juices are thick on his cock, you've never been taken like this before and it's turning you into a mindless creature of need -- you need his cock and you need him to keep fucking you.

He reaches down and grabs a fistful of your hair, pulling you up. "Do you feel that?" he asks, slowing down, his cock rubbing every part of you inside. All you can do is whimper and nod. "This is how you were meant to be fucked," he growls, and all you can do is groan and agree.

He shoves you back down and drills you again and the world starts to spin. Then he slowly pulls himself out of you. You moan at the lack of him and he chuckles, reaching down bodily to lift you up. You lean against his chest with his shirt still on, seeing his pants down around his ankles, feel him move and you know he's kicking his shoes off. He takes you over to the couch's side and drops you, breasts down, onto its wide cushions. The sensation of falling and bouncing complements how you currently feel. And then you're afraid again, afraid that you don't know where he is or what he's going to do next or that he won't do anything at all –

A hand pushes through your hair and pulls you up. You gather yourself onto all fours on the couch's arm and he looks down at you, knife in one hand, cock still hard, deciding.

"Say red now, mistress, or in moments you won't be able to because you'll be gagging on my cock."

Say red? Turn to 105.

Say nothing? Turn to 107.

"Red," you gasp out. "Red, please –"

"Yes, Mistress." He lets go of your hair instantly.

You put a hand to your mouth, and rise fractionally. There's so much you don't understand and can't explain. How can you be so turned on when it feels so wrong?

"I can take you back to the main hallway now. We have extra clothes for you –" he says, looking down at you, eyes that were raging with lust now full of concern.

You shake your head. You don't want to leave yet, you just need space to figure out what's going on.

"It's all so confusing," you say aloud.

He smiles down at you gently. "It's supposed to be."

"I don't get it."

"You don't have to get it. You only need to know if you like it or not." He shakes his head in a comforting fashion. "Not everything is worth examining."

You look around the room again. "So…it's all made up…right?"

He nods slowly. "Everything. My anger, the violence, the knife, all of it." He opens his mouth and you think he's going to go on, then he thinks better of it.

"What were you going to say?" you ask him. "Say it."

His dark smile becomes more perverse and his eyes don't leave yours. "I was going to say that everything's made up – except for the part where I want to fuck the shit out of you." His erection is only barely hidden by his rumpled suit shirt.

You close your mouth and swallow. His admission has a strange effect on you, making your breath speed up a little. He reaches out for your face and slides his hand down it to press fingers into your mouth. It's a debasing experience, this invasion of another one of your soft places. He hooks a finger into your jaw and drags you forward with it like you're a fish he's caught, making you feel oddly possessed. You may have told him slower, and none of this may be real, but him being still in charge is a turn on for you as the growing ache between your legs testifies.

He leans near. "It's not too late to tell me if this is where you want my cock." Then he slowly pulls his fingers out of your mouth.

Do you go back to the main hallway? If so, flip back to 65.

Do you want to continue? If so, turn to 107.

ou look up at him in sheer defiance. "Give it to me."

He growls, looking down at you for a long pause, in which you think this isn't for show, he really is having to control himself. Then he switches grips on the knife and stabs it into the back of the couch and takes your head between his hands.

He doesn't warn you, he just pulls your mouth onto his cock, as deep as he pleases. His cock slides into your throat and down the back of it, and then out again, and he's fucking your face, all you can do is open wide. He grunts each time his head hits the back of you and his hips are swaying in time and his balls are slapping against your chin.

It's awful but it's also good. Being used, being broken down into pieces that aren't a person anymore. You can feel your humanity drifting away, along with all your worries, all your care. You're something primal now, something to use and be used, and you shove a hand in between your legs to play with your clit while he fucks you.

He groans again and you look up just as he looks down. He knows where your hand is. "Did I say you could touch yourself?" he asks you, grinding your face into his cock. It's impossible to speak, but you shake your head. He stops thrusting and leans over, face reflected in the knife. "If you come before I do, I'll cut your fingers off."

His unexpected threat startles you. You drop your hand, and he chuckles, pulling your head off his cock and pushing you onto your back in one smooth motion.

He unbuttons his shirt, one button at a time, then he mounts the end of the couch, his cock pointed at you like a missile – and he takes the knife back up, using it to cut off your soaking underwear.

"Turn over."

You do as you're told, onto all fours, and he pushes you down with one hand. You can feel the point of the blade start at the nape of your neck and then move down your spine, scratching gently along the way. Your ass tightens and your pussy closes, worried about what he'll do next. But his weight behind you shifts, as his knee shoves your legs open. You can feel him lowering himself down on top of you, his cock sliding down the cleft of your ass before finding its home back inside your pussy, making you hiss as he enters you again.

And then he has an arm around your throat with the knife pressed there. All of you stills and tenses, thinking about the knife, except for the hot traitorous part of you inside your pussy getting fucked that wants more.

"Did you think that I couldn't smell the sex on you?" he whispers into your ear. You're pressed so hard into the couch you can hardly breathe, but his cock is pinning you there and it keeps feeling good. "Did you think I don't know what happens here?"

You shake your head, afraid to speak. The fear makes the fucking hotter and you don't want either part to stop.

"Knowing everyone else can have their way with you, without knowing if you'd make it to my door? None of the others have ever asked me to follow them before. Not a one. Watching others have you, take you, having to hold you down on their behalf, not knowing if you'd get – this -- far –" he punctuates each of his words with a deep thrust that makes you moan.

The butler's breath catches, and you can tell he's only barely holding himself back. You don't want him to – you want him to keep going -- the knife against your throat long forgotten.

He smears your sweaty hair out of his way to growl in your ear. "I need to claim you in every hole. Say red now, or I'm going to fuck your ass hard."

Say red? Turn to page 109.

Stay quiet? Turn to page 118.

"*R*ed!" you say before he can take your ass, and he moans as though he's hit a wall.

"Stop, or slower?" he asks, with incredible control.

Slower? Go to 110.

Stop? Turn to 113.

"Slower," you beg him.

"Slower everything?"

"Just slower," you plead.

He pulls out of you and moves the knife away from your neck, throwing it aside. Then he smooths the hair away from your face, watching you closely. Your breath is still coming in gulps and pants, fear and reason warring within. "Trust me," he whispers – the same man who just had a knife on you. But you nod, because you do want to trust him, and your body's still hot with need.

He moves back off of you and helps you sit up, and then turns you collecting you so that you're kneeling, facing the back of the couch, your back to him. You still feel exposed and scared – he doesn't need the knife to tyrannize you anymore.

"Shh," he says, stroking hands down your back. You can hear him moving behind you, and you both know and don't want to know what it is he's doing.

His hands roll down your back and then up both your legs. He reaches up and presses you forward so that you rise up on your knees, making you expose your ass to him. He takes your buttocks one in each hand and spreads them wide and you don't know how much slower he'll be. You're on the verge of saying red, you're scared he'll take you that way when you're not ready, too fast and hard –

When you feel his breath on you there, on your darkest part, you gasp. He stops as you tremble in front of him, and then he breaths on you again.

His tongue finds your asshole and licks gently.

You never would have thought something like that would feel so good. His strong hands knead your buttocks as his tongue strokes again and you find your ass rising up towards him like a cat begging to be pet longer. He leans into you, tongue pressing, hot and moist and he makes the same noises you do half a second later, pleased by your helpless pleasure, and within seconds he's just as in control of you as he was when he had the knife. It would be ironic if it didn't feel so fucking good. Your breathing starts to speed up as his tongue teases your ass – and you know it can't do for you what his cock can.

"Please," you exhale in a rush.

He pulls back just far enough to speak. "Please?" he says, massaging your asshole with his thumb.

You push back towards him, and he laughs low. "Say you want my cock."

"I want it." There's no question that you do.

He moves back and then mounts the couch behind you. His chest against your back, he wraps an arm beneath your arms against your breasts, and you can feel his cock on the cleft of your ass.

"I don't need a knife to own you, do I?" he asks in your ear, rubbing against you, holding one of your nipples in his hand.

You shake your head and he reaches between the two of you to set himself in position.

If he hadn't played with you so long earlier it wouldn't be this easy or feel this good, but because he did you're both rewarded with one long tight slide. You both moan at the same time, and you clutch at the couch's back as he starts his next thrust.

You asked him to go slower, and so he is, taking his time with each arch up and into you before pulling almost all the way out again. His hands are on your breasts, and then one strokes down your stomach to reach between your legs and you shudder as his fingers find you there and start to rub your clit. Everything's methodical, it's as though he's owning you in slow motion. You start to writhe, trapped between his cock and his hand, your clit and your ass begging for him to speed up, but he won't.

"Please," you whisper again.

"Please what?" he whispers in your ear, not stopping one slow thrust.

"Please more," you breathe out.

"More of this?" he says, moving his hand faster, "Or this?" he asks, as he double-times a stroke.

"More of everything," you moan.

He growls and speeds up. He bites your ear and then licks it and then bites his way down your neck as his thrusts increase in speed. His arm around your chest holds you still, massaging your breasts, as his other hand plays your clit harder. You try to reach in but he pushes your hand away – he's in charge of you, knife or not – and it's like he's the captain of a ship guiding you both in. His thrusts speed up and you groan with every stroke that spreads your ass wide and his hand won't stop rubbing you – he's growling now with each stroke, taking control, owning your ass with his cock.

Your body's getting closer, your orgasm winding up. "Please don't stop," you gasp out between strokes, ass tensing, hips hot, empty pussy tight and dripping.

"Never," he growls and bites your shoulder, hard.

You thrash, on the verge of coming, but he bites harder to keep you still – the pain distracts you from the edge coming up until his cock and hand conspire to push you over. Your whole body shakes, your orgasm vibrating out from your core, and he bites harder yet, taking the last of your ass hard to get himself off. You cry out, in pleasure and in pain, and he growls again like an animal, thrusting the last of his load in deep inside you.

You hold onto the couch and to him so that you don't fall down, and you know there's a half-circle of white marks on your shoulder where his teeth have been. Bruises even, maybe – and you know you don't mind.

Turn to page 120.

"Stop," you say, as the fear outweighs the fun.

He pulls out immediately, and lifts himself off of you. "Are you okay?"

You shake your head.

"I didn't hurt you, did I?"

Not in any way you can express. There's not a cut on you, he's been careful so far. It's just that things got too real and too intense and -- you start to cry.

"Oh, Mistress," he whispers, and sounds undone. He throws the knife aside as though it's burned him. "I promise you this was meant to be consensual."

You look away from him, betrayed by your tears. "It just got to be too much."

"I'm sorry. I wanted to push you, but I didn't mean for you to break." He's watching you intently, weighing his next move.

It's a queasy space you're in. You liked being scared – it's why you came this far through the gray doors. You're turned on and frightened and you don't know why they both feel good. "I just – I didn't know."

"I'm sorry," he says. When you don't react, he reaches out his hand and uses a thumb to carefully brush the tears off of your cheek.

Suddenly you're crying hard and you don't know why. Tears well up – sobs, the unattractive kind, and you clamp a hand across your mouth to try to hide them. All the times before in your life whenever you've been hurt or scared, all the pain you ever had and couldn't deal with, the kind you had to put in boxes and close the lids on tight to try to forget – this moment has jostled all of them open.

"Oh, Mistress," the butler whispers again, worried at this change in you. "I'm so sorry, Mistress. I'm so very sorry." He uses his fingers to wipe more of your tears away.

You swallow, take in a gulp of air, and look at him. The concern in his eyes is genuine. And to see so much kindness from someone who moments ago seemed so ready to hurt you – you sob anew.

"My darling, Mistress," he whispers to you, opening his arms. He doesn't dare assume you want him to touch you now, but he wants you to know he's there.

You wipe your eyes fiercely, and crawl across the couch to him, to sit in his lap like a child. His erection is gone, and he takes you in and holds you close to his chest and rocks you, whispering 'Shhhhhhhhhh.' "It's going to be all right," he tells you, when you can breathe.

"How do you know?" you ask him. You feel broken into a million pieces, and you're not sure you can reassemble yourself.

"I'm the butler. It's my job to know," he says, smoothing a piece of your hair out of your face.

From here you can smell the sweat on him that you couldn't before, and the scent of earlier sex still lingers in the room, and your eyes long ago adjusted to the dark. You reach up and touch his chin, where he has what you assume is a 5 AM shadow of stubble, and see his lips curve up into a soft smile.

He bows his head to touch yours. "It's already a little better, isn't it?"

You swallow and nod.

It wasn't the knife that was sharp, really – it was all that standing on the thin edge between trust and fear. But here now, pressed into his chest, fear's receded completely.

He pets your hair again. "I can take you back outside now, if you'd like."

Do you want to go out? If so, turn to page 66.

Or do you want to stay? If so, go to page 115.

ou look up at him and then lean up, to touch his lips with
yours.

"Mistress," he demurs, pulling back, but you follow
him, and your lips land, closed, on his. His hands tighten on you, then
instantly relax, and you know that he's scared of scaring you again.
Beside your outer hip, you feel his cock start to stir.

You kiss his closed lips, and then they part for you as he lets you
lead him. You kiss him, soft and full, probing your tongue into his
mouth, like you've never tasted him before. He stays absolutely still
and you wonder what he thinks of you in this moment. Does he
imagine you a deer, easily startled? Or perhaps you're a cat-wary
dove?

Your lips leave him, but his mouth is still open and hungry.
Beneath your hand you can feel his heart start to pound.

"Mistress," he says again, half-in-hope, half-in-warning.

"It's going to be all right, remember?" you say.

He closes his mouth and nods.

You rise up out of his arms and move to straddle him, sitting
across his lap, facing him. His breath catches, now all hope. You press
yourself into him bodily, kissing him hard, pushing your hands up
through his hair, running your nails on his scalp. His hands hold you
carefully, still unsure.

You move your legs to wind around him, so that there's nothing
between the two of you, and then you reach down between both your
hips to take his cock into your hand. His whole body shudders at this,
and as you move the head of him to graze against your pussy he gasps.

You rise up a little and then let him slide in. His eyes close as you
do and his jaw drops as he moans.

"Mistress," he says to you, his final warning.

This time it's your turn to tell him "Shh."

He rocks up, gently, still afraid of scaring you, as you drop down,
and you meet in the middle. You wrap your arms around his back and
neck, just like your legs are wound behind his waist, and he holds you

closer, like you're something precious to him that he never wants to drop.

He breathes into your chest, lips kissing the edge of your breasts carefully, head bowing with each arched thrust. Each stroke fills you up, and grinds your clit against the skin over his cock. You pull him tighter to you with your legs to get the most out of the friction, as his hands move down to cup your ass so that he can pick you up and then pull you down again.

You bend down to press your head to his as the heat between you grows. He looks up and catches your mouth with his, his kiss full of urgent need.

This was supposed to be a quiet careful fuck, the kind that puts you together, not blow you back apart. But tasting his lips and feeling him inside you and being here inside this House – you start to thrust against him, using him to rub your clit. Whatever baggage you had you've left by the wayside, and now there's only him and this –

His hands reach up to grab your shoulders and pull you down on his cock, hard, with a growl.

"Yes," you hiss, an instruction and a prayer.

He does it again, and it makes you groan.

"Yes, yes, yes –" your words follow the beat of his thrusts into you, as you throb against him, grinding your ever more sensitive clit, until words begin to fail you – you start to throw your head back, ready to come –

And then he's there, reaching up with one hand, pulling your head down, pushing his fingers into your mouth.

"Bite," he commands you – and before you can stop yourself, it's already too late – your teeth close on his fingers, the screaming of your orgasm muffled by his hand.

He grunts in pain but won't stop thrusting, leaving his hand inside your mouth, keeping your head pulled down to watch his face as you feel his cock harden, ready to fill you. You grind your teeth on his fingers and he shouts out, hips high, and you know he's spurting inside. He gasps and sags, each subsequent bob of his hips lower as he sinks back down into the couch. His cock slides out of you as he pulls his fingers out of your mouth. He holds his hand up between you two, and you can see the white-dot semi-circle marks your teeth have left behind.

"See?" he tells you, eyes bright. "You're not the only one who likes to get hurt here."

And you nod.

TURN TO PAGE 120.

ou say nothing and he pulls his cock out of you, and twists you onto your back. He drags your hips up his lap, and puts each of your ankles by his ears and reaches down to set his cock outside your tightest hole, then uses your own juices for lubrication as he slides into your ass.

You whimper – you're not used anal sex so fast or deep, and he slows down instantly, betraying what you were betting on all along, that the violence was all for show. He stills, waiting for your ass to accommodate him, stretching out, feeling good along the way. The pain blossoms into pleasure -- he can read it on your face and immediately starts fucking you again, this time more slowly. Your hips twitch, trying to take him deeper in, and he laughs.

"You need this, don't you?" he says, instead of using you now torturing you with his cock. "You need me in you, or you don't feel whole." He scoops his hips forward, driving deep, and you moan.

He wraps a hand around your thigh and uses his thumb to play with your clit. You gasp and he stops, diving his thumb into your pussy to wet it, and carries on. Everything you've wanted since the room before started with the wax, all of your ache, all of your need, it's like his cock is rubbing on it in you, somewhere deep inside, finding it with every stroke. You're stretched so wide and you've been so abused and you don't know right from wrong anymore, all you know is you want cock – and soon you need to come.

"You want me in your ass," he says, bending forward, rubbing harder on your clit. "Say you want it."

"I want it," you manage to get out. You're moaning with every stroke now, and you're holding onto the couch cushion below you like it might throw you off.

"Say you want my cock," he says, leaning harder, stroking faster, sliding his whole cock in and out of your ass now, pulling it out and then pushing it back in so that you can feel every sweet inch.

"I want your cock," you gasp as he goes back in.

He's curved fully over you now, and you're totally pulled up and exposed to him and his thumb is frantic on your clit and his hips are thrusting against yours, the couch cushion beneath both of you giving way.

"Say you need me," he demands.

You blink up, breathing hard, about to come. You don't want to say anything you don't mean but in this moment, you do need him because without his thumb and his cock and his everything you're so close you've got to-to-to – "I need you!" you scream as you come, your orgasm ripping through your body. You thrash on his cock, muscles spasming inside and out, and you feel his cock go even harder deep inside. He leans forward, everything forgotten but the point where you and he merge, and starts to shout, low and then as loud as you did, as he pounds into your ass. You can feel his cock move inside you like a living thing, filling you up with cum as he gasps overhead.

You expect him to collapse on you after all of that. It's what you would do, if you were in his shoes. But instead he arches back, looking regally down. You hadn't gotten a chance to look at him naked before, what with the knife, but he is a beautiful man. Given the opportunity, you might want to just lie here with him for the rest of the night.

Turn to **120**.

he two of you disentangle yourselves slowly.

Now that he's out of his suit, he's easy to appreciate -- dark skin, wide shoulders, tight stomach and lean arms. Even though you're exhausted – you wish more of all of him would come next.

"I'm sorry to have to leave you, Mistress," he says. "But my job here is done, and I have to go serve my Master now."

You feel your eyebrows rise. "Two things – you have a master? And – this is a job?"

He laughs, and the sounds suits him. "I do have a Master. And this is a job. Albeit one I enjoy."

You frown, not sure if you should feel relieved or pleased or a little like a whore, or even a pimp – then you shake your head. His eyes were real, as were his hands, as was the cock that filled you.

"Where is this Master? Can I meet him?" you ask, as he reaches down to pick up his dropped clothes.

"It's hard to say, Mistress. He comes and goes as he pleases." He offers you a hand, and you stand, slightly shaky.

"What now?" you ask him. You're tempted to lean into him, to think of some way to make him stay.

"There's hours until dawn – and the House has many other doors." He stands in front of you, looking torn, and then reaches for your chin and pulls you in, you think to kiss you, but only to stare deeply into your eyes. "I hope you have a wonderful night here, Mistress."

"Thank you," you say, and he departs.

You sink back onto the couch, naked. Your clothing is trashed and the door you came into this room by is locked to you. You'd panic, but if the Master meant to kill you, well, sending someone to fuck you while holding a knife was already a pretty good chance. You look around and find another door, subtly less black than the rest of the room, something you never would have found in your prior panicked state. You try the key, and it opens, into a majestic and well-lit black marble bathroom – and on it, a tissue paper wrapped package with an outfit folded inside.

You shower, wash your hair, towel yourself off and pull on clothes much like the ones you wore here, underwear, bra, shirt, and skirt. Then you stride across the bathroom and find what you know waits for you there – a keyhole for another door. Prepared for anything, you open it.

Flip to 122.

ou're back in the main hall, but this time the butler isn't there.

Would you like to return to the men behind the purple door? If so, go to 193.

There's still a bath being drawn behind the white door. If you'd like to visit it, turn to page 9.

And walking down the hall you see a door you hadn't seen before – its color is eggshell blue, matching the sky of the nearest painting perfectly. If you want to listen at it, go to 123.

here's a note on the door that you're surprised you didn't see before.

THE SAME HANDWRITING that you saw on the first note that came with the key is scrawled out on the very same stationary.

Have you finished all the other doorways yet?
Perhaps you should.
M

If you want to go back to the purple door with the men behind it, turn to 193.

If you'd still like to take a bath, flip to page 9.

If you'd like to visit the gray doors again, see page 54.

But if you've finished the other doors and want to try your key in this one, go to the next page.

The blue door opens into a bathroom with a shower. You take off your clothes, shower, and then put on a plush robe before opening up the next locked door.

Turn to 125.

$\mathcal{Y}$ou use your key on the door and enter into what at first glance looks like a closet, stepping into it and through a rack of clothing, like you're returning home from Narnia – and you startle a group of older women standing around on the other side. They're all dressed in regular clothing, and very excited to see you.

"You're here at last!" one exclaims, clapping her hands.

"About time," says the second.

"Shush," chides the third. "She's been out and about, having a very good time. Haven't you?" she says pointedly, giving you a knowing look.

You flush from head to toe, and the women laugh. The third one takes your elbow. "Come, come, time to choose."

"Choose what?" you ask her, as she pulls you towards a wall.

"Choose who you want to be," she says, pointing up.

Hung over the wall are six different ornate masks, set with jet and colored gemstones. Wolf, doe, lion, horse, and one set with polished seashells, all of them exquisite.

"Well?" the woman standing next to you says, grinning. "Which one?"

If you choose the wolf, turn to 126.

If you choose the doe, turn to 145.

If you choose the lion, turn to 134.

If you choose the horse, turn to 139.

If you choose the shells, turn to 153.

ou reach for the wolf mask. It's gorgeous, so detailed, the snout ending in a toothy snarl. When you hold it up to your face it perfectly fits. The women smile at you.

"Good choice," one says, and they reach into the rows of clothing all around and produce an outfit for you. They take the mask back from you and cover you in a black sheath dress that reaches to the floor, with a high slit in the side. Then they bring you shoes in your size, strappy black high heels.

"Better not run in these, dear," says one, as she helps you buckle them up. The third is working on your hair, pinning it elegantly up.

"She might run, but she won't get far," says the third, and you want to ask them what they mean, but they're pressing the mask back into your hands. You take it, nervous but curious, and when you fit it up to your face they help to tie it on you. You can see through the perfectly placed eyeholes and turn, catching sight of yourself in a mirror again. You look glamorous – and deadly. The wolf looks wicked – or is that just how much thigh you've got exposed? The only other thing you're wearing is the key around your wrist – and just as you think it, they're pulling you up and over to a wooden door with a slavering wolf carved on it. The door and you match, at least.

"Have fun," the woman nearest you whispers conspiratorially. You inhale, exhale, and use the key to go in.

Turn to 127.

he door opens into an open room, full of men and women, all wearing masks – huddled around tables. You realize slowly you're at a casino, as you see women leaning over tables, throwing dice, hearing mask-muffled cheers. This is not at all where you thought you'd be.

You wander in, looking from table to table. Women wearing rabbit masks walk through with drinks and each drink has a long straw, the better to sip it with from underneath your mask. Foxes in tuxedos stand behind each table, dealing cards. All the male guests are wearing tuxedos too, and the women are all as dressed up as you are. Everyone's masks are almost as fine as yours, feathers streaming, horns curved on display. Those who see you looking at them nod, and you wonder if they know who you are, or are merely being polite.

You come up to a table and watch long enough to gather the easiest rules – those throwing dice, and those betting stacks of chips, are always different people. The betters, men and women, have hands casually rested on their dice throwers hips and asses, sitting back and admiring the view as they push forward stacks of chips.

Figuring this much out you feel accomplished and move along, looking across the room until you see someone from the back, his presence dominating a whole table. As if he feels you looking at him he turns and you see – as he does -- that your masks match.

His chin lifts in recognition and you feel drawn to walk to his side.

The table he's at, the game hasn't started yet, there's a fox beside the board, lining up markers on the felt. The second you reach the table, the others there pull aside, leaving room for you against the other wolf.

He leans in, almost as though he's smelling you, and you can see his dark eyes flicker and take you in from behind his mask. If you hadn't already been through so much of the House to get here, you might not be interested in him so soon – but since you have, it's hard not to imagine the lines of his body underneath his tux, and you're glad those women didn't make you put underwear on earlier.

He smiles – you can see it in his eyes – and wonder if it's a wolfish smile, just like the mask you share.

"Would you roll my dice?" he asks, handing a pair out to you with one cuff-linked hand.

You don't answer but you nod, taking them from him, and turning back to the table where other players wait. Across from you there's a woman in a coppery eagle mask, with a male egret next to her, and a male lion beside a lioness. The egret and the lioness hold dice just like you do – and as the woman in the eagle mask pushes a stack of chips out, the egret leans over to roll.

It's your turn soon. You don't know who's winning or losing yet, you're not sure how to tell, but the numbers that come up please your wolf – you can tell by the way he settles his hand onto your ass – and by how the others push chips towards him, one by one.

It seems like you're winning for a very long time, but you're not rolling to win, you're rolling to keep the wolf near. He's behind you now, his hips following you as you lean forward across the felt, and his hand's found the slit in your dress and is crawling higher and higher up your thigh.

Then there's a commotion at another entrance ahead of you. A group of men all dressed black tuxes with white rams masks have walked in, and they're heading straight for your table. When they arrive, the other players are dismissed.

Your wolf growls at their interruption, but they set down stacks of hundreds of chips, and the fox running the table raises his hands in a gesture of helplessness. Your wolf takes up the dice and hands them to you again.

He makes you roll and roll and roll, and when he's behind you now you can feel his erection pressing in. The rams have one leader, who's taller than the rest, and he's the one who places bets for them, while each of the others take turns rolling.

You still don't know the rules of the game, but you know your wolf is losing, his chips disappear to their side, one by one, until he's reached his last. He holds it up, and then looks at you.

He places it on the table firmly, and then picks you up and sets your ass onto the table's felt. You hear dice roll, feel them land against your ass, and then hear the rams cheer as the wolf growls in defeat. The fox takes your hand and turns you towards the victors, the five male rams – and you realize what the penalty is for losing.

The lead ram takes you in his arms without asking, and carries you off, the other rams following close behind. Your heart is in your throat as you cling to him. He's strong and his chest is wide, and you can see the beginnings of a five-o-clock shadow underneath his mask along his chin. You're breathing faster, scared of what might happen if you're left alone in a room with all of them at once.

"Just you," you whisper. "Just you, not them."

The ram looks down at you. His eyes are blue, and you can see his surprise. He doesn't nod, but you know he heard you, as he pushes the both of you through double doors down a hall, and again into a room. There's a wide bed in the center of it and he throws you onto your back into its middle. Just as you catch your breath again and remember the key, and how you can change the course of things at any time, this is your House – he stands before you at the bottom of the bed. Placing one finger to his lips for silence, he lifts his mask.

He's Nordic, with shoulder length blonde hair and ice blue eyes, and a strong jaw, and lips that are smirking at you, when one of the other rams hands him a wolf's mask -- and you realize you were dealing with a wolf in sheep's clothing all along. You laugh and he grins, settling the new mask over his face – and all the other rams have switched their masks as well, to be gray, blue, white, and tan wolves, the members of his pack. One of them steps forward, and he growls at them, and they step back. To the victor go the spoils – you.

He takes off his tuxedo jacket and tie, throwing them to the floor, and mounts the bed. His erection is straining against his tuxedo pants, and you want to help him set it free.

"Turn over," he says, his voice low.

You know what he wants without saying – it makes sense that it should be like this between wolves. You get on all fours and he slides your dress up, the slit hitching up to your waist now. He grabs your ass and then slaps it, and you know he's left a red handprint behind. You feel exposed, waiting, tight with nerves, as you hear a zipper open and know a cock's been brought out. You tense up, everything stiffening.

The next contact he makes is to play the head of his cock down your ass. He does this a few times, and then drags it down further, and forward, pushing it through your wet labia to nudge at your clit. He holds it with one hand, massaging you there with it. It feels good – you tilt your hips back towards him -- but not as good as you know you'll feel once its inside of you. He pulls back, and you try to follow him, but he holds your hips in place, content to tease. Without thinking about it, you whine. The sound feels right, especially inside the mask. It's how an animal begs for what it wants, and what you want right now is a fucking. The head of his cock finds your clit again, and you whine once more.

At the head of the bed, another of the wolf pack stands. He's unzipped his pants too and lets his erection out, holding it one unmoving hand. You hear pants unzip all around the room as you whine again, pleading to get fucked – and one of the men whines with you. You're not the only one who wants you to get fucked. You whine louder, trying to rub your hips back more, feeling the resistance of his hands, until, and then – the shudder of release as his cock slides home makes you gasp.

The pack around you groan, and start to stroke their cocks as they see you getting fucked. The wolf behind you starts slow, making you feel all of him, teasing the entrance of your pussy with the ridged head of his cock, until you whine again – if that's how you get what you want, then that's how it can be. You whine longer, and the wolf starts to speed up, turned on by your blatant need. Around you the pack stroke faster, by turning your head you can see at least three wolves beating hard cocks. You brace yourself with one hand so you can reach back and stroke your clit.

The wolf mounting you puts up a leg so that he can thrust into you more deeply, and your whines change into grunts. He's got hold of your hips and he's holding you onto him, balls slapping against your clit-rubbing hand, your pussy making wet sounds as he goes in, and you know that all the wolves around the bed can hear and see and smell you getting fucked. It's a turn on that you never thought you'd have, knowing that all these men around you are being controlled by your desire. You're rubbing faster and he's fucking you deep, and one of the other wolves begins to howl, frantically fucking himself with his hand, begging you for release. You rub yourself harder and faster, matching the mounting wolf's pace, and feel your orgasm inside your hips, beginning to grip you. Another wolf howls, and then a third, and a fourth, they're all as ready as you are, and you are, your pussy can't take waiting anymore, all you have to do is rub your clit one...more... time -- you inhale and howl until you're breathless as you come. Your pussy clenches the cock inside it tight, and now your hips are your own, and you're fucking him with them. The wolf mounting you barely manages to hold on, and then he howls himself, hips thrashing wildly into you.

Just as he's filling you up with cum inside, the wolves around you release, their voices loud as silver geysers shoot from their cocks. They stagger onto the bed, finally allowed, as you fall forward onto the sheets, and you find yourself in a tangled pile of half-dressed, cum covered men.

You feel a hand on your ass and cast a lazy glance over your shoulder, where the wolf that mounted you kneels, spent cock draped down one thigh. His mask is half lifted – he doesn't need it to smile wolfishly at you, not at all.

"Thank you, Mistress," he says, and it's echoed by the pack, words, and moans and murrs.

You grin at him, still behind your mask. "I'm just glad I'm bad at dice."

You find the strength to rise up, and hands help you to the ground, a little wobbly on your barely used heels. There's a locked door at the back of the room, and you go to open it.

Go to 132.

The door opens into another bathroom. You disrobe and shower quickly, cleaning yourself up, wrapping yourself up in a robe, and you take your mask with you as you open the bathroom's other locked door with your key.

See 133.

*Y*ou push through racks of clothing again and the women are still there. They're grinning wider this time though, like they know things you don't.

"You're back!" the women exclaim, almost as one.

"How was it?" one asks.

"Don't tell me. I'd be too jealous," says the second. She takes your mask from you and puts it back up on the wall.

"Ready to go again?" the third asks slyly, while you survey the masks.

"Decisions, decisions," you think and say, while deciding. Then you reach for --

If you choose the wolf, turn to 126.

If you choose the doe, turn to 145.

If you choose the lion, turn to 134.

If you choose the horse, turn to 139.

If you choose the shells, turn to 153.

You're distracted by a glimmer behind a rack of clothing. Peeking through, you discover it's a hidden silver door. Do you try to open it? If so, turn to 160.

You reach for the lion mask. It's covered in glittering gold, with an onyx nose, and the eyes are outlined in light green emeralds. You set it onto your face – it's light, and easy to see through. One of the women helps you tie it behind your head and while looking at yourself in the mirror, it occurs to you that you are technically a lioness, since your mask doesn't have a mane.

"Ooh, this is one of my favorite ones," the first woman says.

"Mine too," says the second.

"I agree," says the third. "All that –" she begins, and then looks over at you, grinning. "Roaring," she finishes.

Her tease has given the others long enough to find a gold shift to pull over you. It matches the mask perfectly, and falls down to your knees, and then they bring you matching gold gladiator sandals, which they help you buckle up. You catch your reflection in the mirror and find yourself looking dangerous, glamorous, and fierce.

"Perfection," the first one says.

"Not yet –" the second disagrees, while handing you a massive fur coat. It's heavy, with a wide collar, and it and reaches down to your ankles. You stroke a hand against it, and you can tell that it's made with the finest fur.

"Now it's perfection," the third says, with a strong nod. And then they pull you over to a door with a roaring lion carved onto it.

Turn to 135.

ou walk through a very long well-lit tunnel and emerge into what looks like a cave. Walking forward, you find yourself inside a display of rocks and pavilions like you might see at a zoo, only usually from the other side of the moat that's ahead of you. There's a musty sweet scent in the air, and you realize that this place must have actually held animals in it, once upon a time. You wonder what it holds for you, now.

The pavilion you're on is lit by torches and you're divided from the other half of it by a metal cage. On the other side, two men, naked except for lion masks, lounge on the rocks, stretched out, the torch flame playing off their gilded masks and long, lean, bodies, with manes made of their own flowing golden hair. You walk up to the metal bars that separate them from you, and they spot you, both their matching masks turning your way – they both stand and come as near as they can -- and you realize that they're separated from each other by a gate, too.

There's only one lock in front of you on the bars but it's massive. You set your key into it and turn halfway and metal groans. You thought your key would open up the main door to let them out -- but instead it lifts the gate that separates them from one another first.

The one on the right rushes into the cage of the one on the left. You weren't expecting such sudden movement and you step back, surprised. The one on the left braces as the right one hits him and takes him to the ground, and in seconds they're wrestling. The reason the torch light was so visible on them was because they were covered in oil, they're sliding over one another's bodies, trying to hold one another down. You press your hands to the bars and lean forward, trying to see what's happening, listening to the sound of their blows – it seems like they're fighting over something – and a second later you realize that it's you.

Survival of the fittest, indeed.

"Stop!" you shout out, but they ignore you, one of them has the other's arm behind his back and is driving his chest into the ground.

You put your key back in the lock and finish its whole turn. The gate nearest you lifts and you go in. "I said stop!" you say, running over to them.

They're covered in red welts and forming bruises – their violence was real. They growl and shove apart, kneeling at your feet.

"Which one of us has won, Mistress?" asks the closest.

You weren't thinking about winners or losers watching them fight. They look so similar, especially with their masks on, you can't remember who was coming out on top.

"I was stronger," the other one says.

"But I was faster –" says the other. They look at one another, electricity in the air, and you realize you're seconds away from another fight.

"It was a tie," you say, to calm them.

As one, they both look up at you, and you realize what you've done – they were fighting over you. By stopping them without a clear winner, perhaps they both have an equal claim? Looking down at them, with their muscled backs and arms showing you realize you might not mind that.

"Where?" you ask, your voice lowering.

"Here," the one on your left says, standing quickly. He lifts your fur coat and sets it down on the ground, fur side up. And then the other is at your side, lightly touching your neck, your ear, hands sliding over your dress just as easily as your hands glide down his well-oiled side. The other lion joins you, and together the three of you slip down to the bed of thick fur.

One's at your neck and rubbing your breast, while the other has his hand on your thigh. You feel your dress sliding over your skin, and then that newly exposed skin laying on top of fur which feels incredibly sensual. Their hands are pulling and pushing, your breasts, your belly, your hips. Your dress rises as they work, exposing more of you to the night, and you reach out to touch one and then the other, your hands sliding down their chests over the faint trail of hair on their bellies, leading down to both their cocks.

The one on your right grabs your hips and pulls you over to him, making you slide across the fur. You can tell he's going to be rough but you know you don't mind. The other man snarls at him for stealing you but doesn't fight, as the first lion rises up, cock hard, and then reaches down to set himself into you.

You groan as he pushes in, taking you before you're completely ready for him, creating that delicious friction between desire and need, and he immediately starts to thrust fast, making your body bob against the fur. The other lion leans over and kisses you and then kisses as your breasts as you wind your hands into his hair. Your hips answer the first lion of their own accord, matching his movement with their own, helping him take you. You let go of the second and reach down to touch yourself, rubbing fast, because you know that there's no way the man who's fucking you can keep his pace up – no foreplay, and no restraint, both of you wanting one hard fast fuck.

His stomach curves over you and his hips ram into yours even faster, and you know he's almost done -- and you cry out in frustration and need, because you want it and you're not there yet, but you don't want him to slow down because the friction feels so good.

You feel his cock stiffen and he shouts out and he finishes in you, plunging in deep. And then before he can even soften, he's pulled out and moved away, and the other lion takes his place. His cock is still hard and ready and as he leans forward, you lift up your hips so that your pussy can meet him. Lubricated by the other lion's cum and your need his cock slides hilt deep and both of you gasp once you're joined.

He starts his turn on you, slow sensual thrusts, and despite the fact that their body-types and masks make them look alike, the motions his cock makes fill you in a completely different way.

Now you can take your time with your clit. You do so, rolling your head back on the fur, hips arching up to meet this lion's cock. The other lion lays beside you, spent, watching things intently from behind his mask – and then reaches his hand down to meet yours, to take its place. You moan again, and let him, bringing your hands up to cup your breasts, exposed to the night's air, and he starts speeding his hand up, until he's rubbing your clit as fast as he fucked you, his fingers completely wet, while the other lion continues.

"More, more," you whisper without thinking, as your hips start to bob, and the lion over you growls and starts to speed up. You grab the other lion's hand so he can't move it, because if he keeps rubbing you like that, and the other lion's cock doesn't stop – "More," you beg, like you are in heat, and as one they growl back at you, wanting to make you roar.

"More!" you gasp out, hips high, leaving them arched, as the one lion's hand makes you cum around the other lion's cock. You scream and the lion mounting you thrusts faster into your spasming pussy, and just as you're done shouting he starts, finishing where you left off as he explodes inside of you.

When he's done he slumps over you, trapping the other lion's hand. You wait for your breath to settle, both of them still slick with oil – as slick as your pussy is, filled with both lion's cum.

The stars spin overhead, and you know that eventually they'll be replaced by the unwelcome rays of dawn. You sit up, gently pushing both men away, pulling down your dress, straightening your mask.

"You're right – he's faster, and you're stronger," you tell them, bending down to retrieve your roughly used fur.

The stronger man chuckles at this, as you walk down the rocks and back the way you came.

Turn to 132.

ou reach for the horse mask, and try it on. It doesn't cover your entire face – the ears point up, but the horse's muzzle brims down like a hat that you can see clearly underneath. What's ornate about this one is the mane of horse hair streaming down the back of it, with gemstones braided in. Wearing it you feel high and proud, and one of the women nods strongly.

"Nice, lovely," she says.

"It suits you," says another.

The third sighs. You look at her, hair and beads spilling across your shoulders. "All right, now I'm jealous," she admits.

The others laugh, and start pulling clothing out for you.

THEY DRESS you to match your mask, pulling you into stretchy riding pants, high black leather boots, and a shirt that's so tight it barely covers your chest. Last but not least, they give you a crop.

"You might need this where you're going," one of them says with a wink.

You feel a little sheepish, but let them propel you to a door with a rearing stallion carved into it. You use your key, and then push through.

Turn to page 140.

ou walk through the door and into a dim room. It smells like hay here, and there's hay at your feet. You take a few more steps in and realize you're at the back of a stable, in a stall, alone. You exit the stall and walk down the hall of stalled horses.

A few that are awake whicker at you. You reach out to pet one's velvety nose, and wonder what they make of you in this mask. Soft lips nibble at your fingers, hoping you're holding back a treat. You grin and then you walk on down the row.

There's a final low lit stall at the end with one wall open and a naked man standing inside of it. You can tell from here that his mask matches yours, braids of black horse hair trace down his back. He doesn't hear you as you dip through the struts of the gate to come inside – he's watching what's going on down below.

His stall has a view of a garden set with flickering fairy lights. Distant people look like they're playing tag – and those who've lost are getting fucked on open stretches of green lawn.

He's all alone up here and you wonder if he feels left out. You know you do – especially when the breeze changes and blows the sounds of their pleasure up at you both. You take another step forward, your boot crunches on hay, and he hears you, turning.

What you see next makes you gasp. His cock swings down, almost to his knees – and you wonder if that's why he's been trapped up here, so he can't accidentally hurt anyone. You have no interest in using that thing. If so though, why are you also here? And why do you share the same masks?

His skin is light, except for on his cock where it's a ruddy red. He's built like the horses you just walked by, arms thick, thighs tight with muscles. The look on his face is more wild though. The only other thing in the stall with you both is a tack box. You move over to it without taking your eyes off of him and open it. Lights inside turn on, illuminating a bag of sugar cubes, a bottle of lube, and a strap-on. You look down at your outfit – you may wear a horse mask, but you're dressed like a rider.

"Come over here," you command. He walks over to you, hesitant, eyeing your riding crop, wondering just what kind of rider you'll be.

You reach into the tack box and grab a sugar cube, offering it to him. He takes it like a horse might, his lips soft on your fingertips, looking at your face, your chest, and your hips, and his gargantuan cock starts to go hard.

You still want nothing to do with that – but you are interested in him. You know what it's like to feel left out, looking in, and you enjoy being kind. You place a hand on his chest, feel his skin twitch beneath it in equal parts surprise and hope, and stroke down him like you might a stallion's side.

Moving around him, you pull your hands back up his chest and over his shoulders, and down his back, key dragging along behind. His muscles are so well defined it's easy to trace their outlines, so you do, working your way one muscle at a time until you reach his ass which clenches, trembling a little beneath your hand.

"Don't be scared," you whisper to him, like you might encourage a horse. You play the head of the riding crop against him dragging it down his spine, then change, swinging it down to pull it up the cleft of his perfect ass. He rises up on his toes then sighs, tilting back as he trusts you more, as he begins to have desires.

You move around to be in front of him, and take another sugar cube up. His eyes are full of challenge for you, the steel of his jaw set, and yet you make him bend, making his lips follow your hand.

Three sugar cubes later, and he's on all fours on the floor. The sheer weight of his cock makes it dangle almost to the ground – you stroke a hand down his back and sides, moving with the contours of his body so that he knows where you are, as you reach your hand in to feel his girth. He shivers at your touch, and you find his cock is hard, and he arches his ass up as you stroke it. He's ready – but are you?

You stand and go back over to the tack box. The strap-on is only half as long as his cock is, but just as hard, black silicone without much give. You buckle it onto yourself, front and back, and squirt lube into your hands to warm it before stroking it up and down the silicone cock like it belongs to you.

Then you turn back to the horse-masked man, his mane streaming across his back, his ass facing you, waiting to add his sounds to the music of those already fucking below. You get down on your knees, scuffing the toes of your boots, and crawl near, steadying yourself on his ass with both hands as you aim the strap-on at him.

You set just your tip inside at first. His whole body tenses and shakes. You stroke your hands down his back and ass, and up his thighs, as you slide slowly deeper, then back out again, warming him up.

You don't know anything about men's asses, but you do know yours, you know what you like, and giving it to him seems the most obvious course. You stroke again, going a little further, watching his ass spread to take you in, hearing him moan.

"Do you like that?" you ask him, stroking another hand down his back. He doesn't answer you but his thighs open wide, allowing you deeper access. As you speed up a little you're surprised to find that the strap-on curves up to rub against your clit, even through your riding pants. You thrust into him again and feel it stroke you, as you stroke him. His back arches, his ass opens, and you begin ride him.

Your strap-on slides deep into his ass, completely disappearing there, making him grunt as it lands home. It rubs your clit on each stroke in and each stroke out, giving you incentive for greater friction, but you don't want to come alone. You slow yourself, and he moans a complaint, until you bend over him and reach down.

The weight of his dramatic cock makes it almost slap the ground. You wrap your fingers around it, and he gasps as you gently pull along his shaft.

"Do you like this?" you ask him,

He doesn't break character and speak, but he strongly nods.

You let go of him, and place your hands back on his ass, burying the strap-on deep. His back is wide, so it's possible to lean on him – you reach out with one hand to catch a hank of mane, and realize it's been braided into his long hair, as his head rears back. Without think-ing, you pull and grind yourself in, and he grunts as you find new depths inside. You spin your hips in a circle, making the strap-on rub you hard. When it starts feeling good, when his ass is nice and wide, you pull back on his hair a second time with one hand, feel him shudder on you, pinned – and with your other free hand you reach for his heavy cock.

It wouldn't be possible if he wasn't so strong, you couldn't balance on him any other way, but he can take it, what's more is he wants it, he opens up every time that you lean in, your hips thudding rhythmically into his, the end of the strap-on grinding against your clit with every stroke you give his ass – and then his cock. You're amazed at the girth and length of it, it's hard for you to reach his head, but you stroke what of it you can reach, feeling it harden under your ministrations like a cannon getting ready to go off. He leans forward to give you more of his ass and you take it, rising up on your feet instead of knees, so that you can land harder into him, the strap-on plunging in time with your breath, and his breathing starting to become one extended moan. The horses in the stalls behind you are whickering, awakened by your noises and your scent, like they're encouraging you to mount him harder. Your hips slap against his ass as it rises higher still, him grunting every time he takes you in, your clit rubbing so hard against the strap-on's end, and underneath you both the pendulum of his cock as it's swung by your force and hands, keeping ever faster time.

You reach the point where coming will be involuntary, where there's no way to hold back. You let go of his cock and put another hand in his hair and pull tight on it like reins as you take what you need from his ass, pounding wildly into him so that the strap-on will rub your clit just right. You cry out as you come and ride it through on him, translating all of your waves of pleasure into three more deep hard thrusts, and stay there, curved against him, collapsed against his back, ass deep.

"Hold on," he warns you, speaking for the first time. You grab hold of his thick shoulders as he bucks up and both his hands leave the floor. They start working his thick cock desperately, as it rises like a snake, his ass throbbing from your dildo still inside. You've never seen a cock before that requires two hands, and you realize you might never see one again, as he uses them in conjunction, stroking up his magnificent staff, hilt to head, as if drawing up the cum.

His ass twitches, you feel it do so, telegraphed to your clit, and then he shouts out loud, while still stroking hard. Cum jets out, spewing up then back down over down over his hands and shaft like he's uncapped a fountain. His whole body shivers and shakes, muscles spasming, as he works the last of it through, greasing his own cum up and down his length. Then he sags forward onto all fours, as though all of his strength has just poured out of his cock. You brace and pull back slowly, and he moans as he feels you leaving his ass. You stagger to standing behind him, your conquered mount. Undoing the buckles keeping the strap-on in place, you set it carefully back into the tack box, and pull the bag of sugar cubes out.

When you turn towards him again, he's still catching his breath on the stall floor, the wet tip of his cock lying in the hay. He looks up at you, eyes still defiant. You may have ridden him into the ground, but he's still wild inside.

"Good stallion," you murmur, offering three sugar cubes out, stacked on your hand. He smirks, bows his head, and eats them, soft lips grazing your palm. Then you stand, and walk back down the line of stalls. One of the horses inside calls to you, and you turn towards him. His lips are pulled back so he can catch your scent. He knows fucking and the recently fucked when he smells it, and his cock releases from his sheath, aroused.

"Good stallion," you tell him too, setting your bag of sugar cubes on the ledge of his stall. Then you turn and spot another door.

Turn to 132.

ou lift up the doe mask. It's not as fancy as the others but it has an unearthly shine, because, you realize as you pick it up, it's inlayed with topaz of every shade, mosaicked out in the semblance of a female deer. The work behind it is extraordinary – you feel like if you put it on you might never take it off. Turning to the mirror, you raise it to your face. It covers you, forehead to chin, but it isn't claustrophobic, and you tie the ties behind your head without thinking.

"Ooh, that one's fine," says one of the women, appreciating your choice, before heading towards the shoe-rack.

"I love this one's dress, just hang on," says the second, also disappearing.

"The dress is no good without these," says the third, holding out garters and stockings. She pulls off your robe before you can complain and fastens the garter belt around your waist, then kneels to assist you with the hosiery. They have Cuban seams, black lines that follow up the back of your legs which she's evened out expertly just as the second woman returns.

She's holding a light brown dress up that's so swingy it looks like a wave. It's perfectly form-fitting – you know, because they're pulling it on you, even over the mask -- but as soon as it reaches your waist it flares out, swinging in all directions down to your knees. You spin because it's the kind of dress that requires spinning, and the skirt flares, showing off your hose's seam.

The first woman reappears again. "Shoes!"

They're brown, but they're just as bejeweled as your mask. You let her slide them onto your feet, and even though everything is brown you feel a little bit like Dorothy and a lot like Cinderella. They're comfortable -- you feel like you could dance in them all night, and say so.

"That's very convenient," the first one says, pulling loose strands of your hair back, tucking them in with a golden pin.

"Treat the Master nicely, will you? And tell him we say hi?" says the second one.

"Wait – what?" you ask, but the third's shushing her and propelling you towards a door with a leaping stag carved onto it.

You look back at them. Their smiling faces betray nothing, and you get the feeling they won't tell you anymore, so you reach for your key.

Turn to 147.

$\mathcal{B}$ehind the door there's a long tunnel which gives you too much time to think.

It makes sense that there's a Master here, somewhere, but you hadn't planned on meeting him. If you do see him, what will you say? Anything you can think of would be awkward. He knows what you're doing here – he must, of course, since he planned it all for you – but you're not sure you could publicly thank him for it. Or privately, for that matter.

There's another door at the tunnel's end and you can hear music playing behind it. Still wondering what you'd say or do, you push it open.

The tunnel's brought you to a place that only movies have prepared you for – you're clearly at the edges of a masked ball. Massive chandeliers hang overhead, and there's a small orchestra playing music at the edge of a wide parquet dance floor.

Everyone there has a full mask on, just like you, although everyone's masks and outfits are different. There's a woman with a tiger mask on and an orange Marie Antoinette dress, like she's queen of the French tigers. A man is all dressed in black and wears a mask with a green dragon's face and curving red horns. No one matches, and everyone is on the dance floor, where people meet, dance, and part again, according to the song.

How would you know the Master, even if you did see him? You must admit, now that those women put the thought in your head, you are curious. Looking around, you see there's no one else here dressed as you are and your dress is one of the simpler ones, although if your mask shines like your shoes do, you know that you are glowing.

A man in a raven mask puts his hand out to you and you take it, letting him pull you out to the dance floor. There's a fine edge of feathers around his neck, which tickle up under your mask as he pulls you near. He's an expert dancer, easy to follow, which is good because you don't recognize the song.

You're just about to ask him if he's the Master when he stops dancing, separating from you to bow low. The music's stopped too, but you didn't feel the song end – you feel a tap on your shoulder, and turn.

A man stands there. He's taller than you are – and made taller still by his mask of a stag with a full rack of horns. All of his mask glitters in the light, covered in topaz and diamonds, right out to the horn's gold gilded tips. The rest of his clothing is old fashioned, a fluttering collar revealing collarbone and breeches tucked into what you can only assume are deerskin boots.

Saying nothing, he bows, and you bow to him in turn. You realize the entire room's gone still and silent, watching you both.

This then, you realize, is the Master.

By an unseen cue the music begins playing again and the stag-masked man holds his hand out to you, asking you to dance with him. You take his hand and daintily step inside the circle of his arms.

The mask is saving you from the flush of embarrassment tinting your cheeks and from the obligation of speaking. He's willing to lead, all you have to do is follow. He moves so smoothly, you know that even if you misstep no one will know. Your skirt flares out as you both turn, slapping against both of your legs, like it's trying to pull him nearer to you.

This is different from the other paths you've traveled here. His arms are strong as they guide you around the dance floor, but every-thing feels oddly…chaste. Which wasn't how you expected the Master of the House to be, at all.

He moves you through the space that other couples make, taking you all over the dance floor, as the song you're dancing to begins to wind down. It has a seductive refrain which echoes, giving him an excuse to pull you close. You run a hand up his back to hold on as he dips you low three times, spinning before each, making you dizzy in a very good way. Then he sets you right again, holding onto you as the music ends until he's sure you've found your feet, looking down into your eyes through the holes in his glorious mask. Underneath your hand his chest rises and falls, betraying the effort it requires to look effortless.

That's your moment – your chance to say something to him that only he can hear. You pause, trying to think of what to say, but words escape you. He separates from you and gives you another bow, before standing and walking away.

The man who's planned all of this for you, for reasons you can't even begin to comprehend, and all he wanted was one solitary dance.

The music starts again and the crowds merge and begin to choose dancing partners. Despite the height of his mask if you don't act soon he'll be out of the room and what then? You run after him, pushing through people, glittering heels clattering on the wooden floor.

You can't even call after him to tell him to wait. That feels like it would be too much. But you catch up to him, and reach out for his arm, just before he's about to step off of the floor. He pauses at this, and looks down at your hand, before looking at you.

Actions speak louder than words here, what with the music rising and your masks on. You let your hand slide down his forearm to his hand and pull him gently to you, back to the dance floor. He pauses, then takes a step, and another, until he's right beside you. You position your arms like they were when he held you earlier, and he fits near you once again.

This time the dancing doesn't stop when you both regain the floor, so while the song is slower, he has to avoid the other couples. His hand is at your waist and hips, then back, his feet guiding you both, always keeping you close. He smells lightly of sweat and of soap and the shirt he's wearing is thin enough for you to feel his muscles underneath it. You tilt your head so that you can rest it on his chest as the song slows, and imagine you can hear his heart beating. One of his hands travels up your back to press you into him – the great mask above bows, and you can look up and see that his eyes are closed contentedly.

Does he know what you look like, underneath this mask? Does he know what this night's explorations have done for you – have meant to you? Your whole world's been turned upside down and changed, all because of him.

When the song ends you don't let him go. His eyes open in surprise, but he only tries to release you for a fraction of a second before gathering your intent. As if the musicians are sensing your mood, the new song is slower, its beat more deliberate.

You don't know any of these other people and they don't know you. They can't even see you, not with this mask on. But you feel like you know him, having walked through so many of his doors. You raise your arms up and loop them around his neck, pressing your entire body close.

His hands are hesitant at first, unwilling to take advantage of you. But when his dark eyes meet your serious gaze, they stroke down from your ribs to your hips and pull you closer as he takes you traveling in wide circles.

Speaking seems verboten – no one else is – and besides, you no longer want to talk. You let your hands travel up his neck, running your fingernails on his scalp in between his mask-ties, and he reacts, hands tightening. The music thrums and you grind yourself into him. He reacts to that too, you can feel his erection start to swell inside his breeches. You sink your hands down his back, tracing nails down his shirt until you've got your hands on his hips too, and you pull him closer as you rise up on your toes, curving yourself up against him.

You didn't know what you were going to do until just now, but now that you've thought of it, there's no turning back.

You raise up a leg and loop it around him. His nearest hand grabs your hip to pivot you in time with the song, then slide lasciviously up your thigh. You do nothing to discourage him, as he takes your ass in hand, and then you're both standing there, you half wound around him with your glittering shoes. Pressed hip to hip, you listen to him breathe, your own breath sounding loud inside your mask. The dance floor has narrowed down – there are other couples on it but they hardly matter, for both of you it is just you two.

You'd be willing to follow him off of the dance floor if he pulled you there – you're hoping that he will, and you're so glad you just have a garter belt on underneath – but instead his hands find your hips again and he's pulling you up. Your other leg swings up naturally and suddenly his entire torso is between your thighs. You lock your feet behind him as he dips you again, skirt fluttering down.

When he's done with the dip he doesn't let go and you don't want him to. You pull your skirt up, exposing the seams of your lovely thigh-high hose, and then reach down between your own legs to his pants. At feeling your hand on him, even through fabric, he gasps – the first noise either of you has made in the presence of the other. And that seals it. You unfasten his breeches and reach in to find him firm and aching, and before you can think about it, what it means to get fucked here by him with so many other people in the room, you've canted your hips and set him in position outside your pussy and he's slowly sliding in.

Your legs tighten as you feel him enter you, and your hands reach for his shoulders, holding yourself up, and holding on, as his strong arms sink you. You make a small sound as he slides home, filling you completely, like this was how you were meant to be. Dancing's forgotten, this is the only thing that matters, this point of honest unmasked contact between you two.

He moves you on and off of him, your flowing skirt hiding the penetration happening underneath. Anyone dancing nearby would know, but they don't matter, not like he does, not like you do, his hands cradling your ass, picking you up, settling you back down, on and off of his cock in time with the band.

You can't touch yourself because you don't want to let go, but also because you like being taken and helpless. You close your eyes and fold in, giving into sensations, feeling him inside of you, the louder rhythm of the music, the speeding breath of his chest. It doesn't matter what anyone else can see – they don't know you, they just know you're getting fucked by him. The thought frees you to moan and as you do so he speeds up. You cling tighter to him, your skirt swaying with each of his thrusts, and you moan again. His breath is coming faster now, and inside his mask you know his jaw is dropped. He's not only pulling you on and off of him, but he's swaying to thrust more too, filling new places inside of you with his cock. Your hands tighten at his shoulders, holding on for the ride, breath catching with each stroke. You're not going to come but you don't care because it feels so good to make him lose control – he may be the House's

Master, but you're the one who's mounted him – you start to make high pitched sounds and he growls inside his mask, his hands almost bruising you. You feel his cock inside you stiffen harder and as the music reaches a crescendo he grinds you into him, your hips bound by his hands, you both swaying as he thrusts like you are still dancing as he loses himself inside of you with a long guttural groan.

Still transfixed, you hold on, eyes closed as you relax against his chest. He's panting but he keeps you in place, holding you more gently now. It's his turn to wait until he's not dizzy, and then he carefully pulls you up and his cock slides out of you, and wetness gushes between your legs. Reaching down, you set him back into his pants again, leaving the fastening of his pants undone. You set one leg down and then the other, and as your skirt falls down into place, standing feels brand new. The other couples still circle the dance floor, willfully ignorant of what just went on. His chest is still heaving as he looks down at you. You smile up at him, then realize he can't see it, so you lift up the hem of your skirt and curtsy low.

He steps back and bows regally to you, equally solemn.

And then you walk off of the dance floor alone.

Turn to page 132.

ou lift the mask of shells off the wall. It hides little, just your eyes, and can be tied behind your head with just one string.

"Who's going swimming?" the first woman asks with a cheerful clap.

"But I didn't bring a suit –" you protest, as the second woman clucks.

"You should always be prepared for a pool party," she says.

The third emerges from the back. "Luckily, we plan ahead –" she says, holding up a black two piece swimsuit with metal rings at the hips and the corners of the top. "Come on now, out of that robe."

They descend on you and help you pull the swimsuit up and on, tying it perfectly around you. You don't feel like you could swim a marathon, but it also doesn't feel like it's going to crawl up or fall off, which is pleasant.

"Is there anything else I should know?" The other masks have all lent themselves to particular feelings and themes – and so far this one leaves you the most exposed.

"Yes – ignore anyone who tries to give you wax," the first one says with a wink.

"That's not very helpful –" you begin, but it's too late, the second one's already pulled you to stand in front of a door covered in waves, with a splashing mermaid's tail.

Turn to page 154.

ou realize that you're barefoot too late, after the door's already closed behind you. The floor under your feet is patterned cement and you're inside a short tunnel. Up ahead you can hear music and fountains and you walk towards them.

You emerge outdoors. It's still night and you can see the stars above. Lamps that look like glowing jellyfish light a path to an enormous organically shaped pool. It looks like a lagoon and has several islands with waterfalls inside of it. Women in mermaid outfits are singing on one of them.

Other people – servants? Guests? – walk around the pool's edge, and men and women in fox and rabbit masks carry trays of drinks around. Everyone has masks on, but their swimsuits leave little else to the imagination. A woman in a rabbit mask wearing a tight one-piece suit brings you a drink. You take it and begin a stroll around the pool.

Several of the mermaids are sitting on an island in the middle of the pool brushing one another's long hair, while others are lounging on rocks looking up at them, breasts cupped at the water's edge, finned tails dipping in and out of the inky water. The ethereal song playing is hauntingly beautiful, adding to the atmosphere of the dark water and swaying lights. It's hard not to stare – even though you know they're just people in costumes, they look like renaissance paintings come to life. You can see their lips moving in time with the music, and when one of them splashes another and she laughs melodically, you realize they're not just lip-synching, that they really are singing the song.

One by one they drift away from the island and out into the pool, swimming faster with their tails than a normal person could without, their hair streaming behind them in the water. The reappear, splash, play, and sing, and then swim back, strong arms pulling themselves up onto the rocks again.

One of them sees you watching her and instead of staying with her sisters, she nears.

Her body is a barely visible hourglass under the water's edge, her hips curving out then legs pulled tight by the tail she wears. It's sewn with sequins, you can see them glitter in the light. She smiles up at you and you helplessly smile back – then she takes in a mouthful of water and spits it at your feet in play.

You dance back and she laughs and then you're laughing too. Her waist-length black hair is wet, slicked against her head before it clouds out around her in the water. Her eyes are large and beautiful, perfectly framed by long wet lashes, and the lips that just spit water at you pout.

"What?" you ask her lightly.

She shakes her head. Like the others, you doubt she's supposed to speak. And yet.

"Did you need something?" you ask, kneeling down, holding your glass in one hand.

She thrashes her tail, rising up in the water, letting you see her floating breasts. She's topless, like some of the others, and her nipples are small dark moons.

You lean closer, entranced, and quicker than you thought she could, she rises up to kiss you. Her lips meet yours and in your surprise she puts her arms around your neck and pulls you in.

Compared to her you're ungainly, and you splash into the water like a cannonball. "Hey!" you shout as you emerge, treading water. You can't touch the bottom, so you know it's deep. But the water's warmer than you thought it would be, as is the steadying hand on your arm and the sweet laugh in your ear. You turn and find her right beside you.

"You got me wet –" you protest, straightening your mask. The pool's saltwater, you can taste it in your mouth.

She tilts her head in a way that lets you know *she* doesn't mind. She swims a little nearer, beating the water by your legs in a steady rhythm with her tail.

"If you'd wanted a drink, you could have just said so." Your glass is now somewhere at the bottom of the pool.

Her eyebrows raise in a way that makes you think about all the other things that she might actually want. Suddenly you are wet, and not just from the water.

A wicked smile plays over her lips, perhaps sensing the change in you. And when she leans closer this time to kiss you, your lips part.

The water makes your hands slide over her skin, and seems to attract them to dangerous places. Her breasts press up against yours, and her hand is at your back, undoing the ties to your swimsuit there. You gasp and look up – you might care, but everyone else seems far away – she's pulled you out to the center of the lagoon, and out here the water's too dark for anyone else to see – which is good because one of her hands has settled on your hips and is stroking down your belly.

You kiss her again underneath the stars. The other mermaids are still singing and now that you're in the water, it's like they're singing for you. Your tongue presses deep, and then you want more. You pull back and kiss the wet line of her jaw, her neck, hold onto her with one hand as though she might try to get away, and dive underneath the waterline to find her nipple with your mouth. Her hands play in your hair, and the mask unties, sinking down to join the top of your bathing suit and glass in the dark.

You rise up and she's breathing heavily, kissing you again, hands on your breasts, rubbing against them before rolling your nipples. The water makes everything either of you do electric, each wave a current shared between only you two.

Her hands circle your waist, and she starts to pull you out into the lagoon. You let her, holding to her side, amazed at how fluidly she moves, how delicious it feels to be skin against skin, until together you reach the island in the center.

She pushes away from you and mimes breathing in deeply. You follow her lead – and then she pulls you under the water again.

Your legs kick alongside her tail. Your eyes are open but the water here is dark black and frightening. Her hair feels like seaweed and you remember too many myths about mermaids pulling men in to drown.

But you're not a man. And just before you panic about running out of air, you and she bob up into what you realize is the center of the island, a hallowed out cove. There's a small skylight you can see night through and the music of the other mermaids singing outside echoes as water trickles in.

What's more, is your feet can reach the bottom here, the side's lined with stairs to a very shallow pool. You stand and walk up a few stairs, breathing sweet air in deep.

When you're done being frightened, you look back and find her still in the water, arms sweeping, breasts high. You take a step down to her. She smiles, and you take another step.

She meets you as soon as your hips reach the water line again. Her hands stretch up your body, asking for more of you to touch, and then she's pulling the bottom of your swimsuit off, exposing you to her. You gasp, and she stops, but then you step down the final step so that you're swimming beside her again, nakedly.

You feel the water move as she does, her lips on yours, her breasts sliding wetly against your own, and you feel one of her hands slide down your side and between your thighs as you kick the water to stay up. You let yourself sink into her, gulp in air, dive down to kiss her breasts and ribs, feeling the water move between you both. As her fingers rub and dip into you rise up again to gasp for air. She smiles at the power she has over you, and pulls out to grasp your hips hard, pushing you back until the stairs are under your feet and at your back. She forces you to sit down, and then spreads your knees wide, and ducks down to lap at you.

You groan, the sound hidden by the mermaids singing above. Her head is in your lap, chin just under the water line. Coming up for air, she grins at you, and your pussy misses the warmth of her tongue.

"More," you whisper. She grins wider now and dives back down.

Her tongue strokes clit, then your folds, and then licks your pussy open to press in. Her whole body moves with each stroke of the tail she's beating under the water to stay afloat, pushing her tongue harder into you wherever it touches, insistent like a beating heart. Cool air blows in and chills you where she's not shielding you from it, and you wish you were touching more of her – her tongue is amazing, but the rest of you wants her heat too.

You sit up and stroke your hands down her back where you can reach, until your fingertips find her costume's seam. She stops bobbing up and down and you hear her breath catch.

You stroke one fingertip underneath the edge of the seam along her waist until you find a zipper on her hip. You start it at the top and then with your hands push it down and open.

She looks up at you, eyes wide, as you expose her hip and her ass, scooting down now to push more of the fabric off of her. She twists in the water and lets you, helping you, until she swims back out of the end of the costume, as naked as you are, and free. You set the costume on the stair beside you.

"Does this mean you're a selkie?" you ask her.

Still in character, if not in costume, her lips pucker impishly and she swims in. You lean down to kiss her, only instead of her pulling you into the water, this time you're the one pulling her out of it, up the stairs, hands hot on one another, sliding over curves and into secret places, mouths locked, until you reach the shallow pool at the stair's top, and kiss across it until you've got her pinned against the cove's wall.

You sink to your knees and push her thighs apart and kiss her where she was just kissing you. Her clit rolls beneath your tongue. She moans and it echoes in this small place, and you want to make her moan harder, until the singing overhead can't overcome the sound. But then she's kneeling too, kissing your mouth again, and you're in a tangle of slippery warm limbs, kissing one another's breasts and stomachs until you're both lying side by side, and it seems only natural to place your head on her thigh as she's done on yours, so that your tongue can reach her just as she's reaching you.

You kiss her labia in turn and then press your tongue in, her salty sweetness tasting not unlike the water nearby. As your tongue strokes her clit she moans again, that sound that you want her to make more of – but then she's licking you too and it's your turn to moan. She purrs into you, pleased by your pleasure, and then you both begin, trying to make the other person come first like it's a game. Her fingers enter you as her hips thrust and you thrust back and everything you're doing to one another is like being part of a perpetual motion machine, rocking and kissing and licking and pushing fingers inside, each move returned to its owner tenfold. It's hard not to cry out only that would mean taking your mouth off of her, and more than anything else you want to feel her shudder when she comes, knowing that you gave that her that pleasure.

Your pussy starts to clench around her fingers just as she starts to moan without ceasing, and you feel her orgasm winding up inside of her just like yours is winding inside of you, and you hold her hips harder with your free hand, trying to make sure that you can ride her out in the same way you want to be ridden –

She comes a second before you, her moan in your pussy turning into a scream that not even the sirens overhead can hide. Her fingers spasm inside of you and her mouth is hot and her juices in your mouth are sweet and suddenly you're coming too, body writhing as she drags you in all over again, shouting just as loud. Waves flow through you both as you keep lapping, moans turning into quieter sounds of pleasure, until you fall apart, exhausted.

She rises up before you do and kisses you with lips that taste like yourself, before pointing out a hidden keyhole in the wall. Then she smiles widely, steps down to where you left her tail, picks it up, and dives back into the dark water below.

You lay in the shallow pool for a bit listening to the mermaids sing, watching the stars above, before standing and using your key to reveal an elevator door.

Turn to page 133.

he women cluck. "Are you sure, Mistress?" says the first one.

"I forget, did you already try all of the masks?" says the second.

"Once you go through there, you can't come back anymore," says the third. "If you go through that door, the night's nearly done."

"Are you *sure* you tried out all the masks?" the second one encourages you again.

You look back at the wall of jeweled masks again and then over at the door.

If you choose the wolf, turn to 126.

If you choose the doe, turn to 145.

If you choose the lion, turn to 134.

If you choose the horse, turn to 139.

If you choose the shells, turn to 153.

If you're determined to press on, turn to page 161.

"I want to press on," you say. They sigh dramatically, but move the rack of clothing aside – you hadn't realized it was on wheels before. There's a wall of silver behind it – you realize that it's an elevator door. There's no buttons to call it, just an escutcheon for your key.

"Where does it go?" you ask.

"Onward," says the third of them, while the other two are quiet. "After this point, you can't go back again. There's not enough time."

Which was what you were afraid of. You look at the masks, carefully rehung on the wall, and feel the weight of the rich robe you're in, and your body remembers all the hands that have touched it tonight, the places they've reached, the pleasures you've had. You're not ready to give all that up just yet.

And…yet…you still want to know what's waiting for you.

You look around to the women. "Thank you. For everything."

"Of course," the first says, smiling.

"Our pleasure," the second says, with a grin.

"Your pleasure, more like," the third says, with a snort, then smiles and tilts her head towards the elevator door. "Go on, girl. You know you want to."

You do want to. And so you step up, and press your key in.

IT TAKES thirty seconds for the elevator to arrive, long enough for you to have second, third, and fourth doubts. But when its doors open, revealing a plush carpeted and wood paneled interior, you feel brave all over again. You step inside, and wave good-bye to the women as the doors close.

The elevator moves so smoothly you almost can't sense it, and it's an honest surprise when the doors open to show you somewhere you haven't been before. You're in a room that looks gilded with gold, and you step out, onto golden tiles, into what appears to be a museum floor. There are paintings set all around, and you look up and behind you and discover that the elevator you just exited from is part of the pedestal of a giant statue. You don't recognize it until you're a few steps back and can take it all in – it's Leda and Zeus, him taking her as a swan. She's in marble, arms swept back, face ecstatic, legs wide, as the swan, also marble, flutters open-winged overhead, neck bent mid-bugle. It feels like an oddly fitting choice when you start to look around. There are paintings from floor to ceiling here, more nymphs and satyrs, shepherds and shepherdesses, skirts high, ready to run from one another in a game of immortal tag, the entire museum dedicated to showcasing ancient acts of love.

You walk over to the first painting and find it eerily realistic. It's set back into the wall so that you can't touch it, but you feel like the men and women in it are alive. It's the same for the second, and the third, their subject matter similar, only the skin tones of their subjects different.

You stand in front of the fourth one and watch it, you've almost made a circuit of the room, and you don't know what you should do next, all of the other rooms were self-evident.

Then you think you see a satyr wink.

You take a surprised step back, and one of the nymphs, a willowy blonde, smiles.

Then a third one moves, reaching out to touch the man she's chasing, and he moves to turn towards her, and the figures in the painting have come alive – stepping down from elaborately constructed alcoves and out from behind painted canvases that seemed to be their clothes. A masterful use of forced perspective and your own gullibility made the paintings look flat, but now that the gig is up, everyone inside the paintings is joyously alive – and pouring out to meet one another.

The satyr now exposed, his pants a fabrication of the diorama he was in, reaches for and catches the nearest girl. She squeals and falls back into him, her clothing half painting, and half a series of sheer scarfs she had tied around neck and waist. Two girls that were about to step into a painted river step into one another's arms instead, mouths meeting hungrily. You hear feet on tile and look around to see the other painting's occupants moving, falling into one another's arms, pleased laughter and the sound of moans, and you realize this room's point.

It's an orgy.

You're in front of the elevator shaft again, framed overhead by Zeus's great wingspan. The door is still open, you can head back inside.

Do you leave? If so, turn to page 165.

Do you stay? If so, turn to 166.

ou shake your head. You don't want to interfere, you just want to see her, hear her, feel her shake the bed as she lets her orgasm go. At your refusal she closes her eyes and falls into the pleasures the redhead is giving her again, and your lips part as hers do, your breath catches as you see her ribs rise, and it's so easy to imagine yourself being her, underneath the redhead's insistent tongue – when the darker woman cries out your jaw drops and you gasp with relief for her, for you both. You hadn't even realized you were holding your breath, but you were.

The black woman sinks back on the bed, and reaches her hands down to run through the rising redheaded woman's hair. The redhead looks at you.

"Are you sure?" she asks, an invitation.

If you're not sure about just watching anymore, turn to 186.

Or perhaps you turn your head and think you see a shadow inside one of the white fabric columns beside the bed. If so, turn to 41.

hat many people, and that place – it just wasn't for you. The elevator's doors close in front of you, taking you away. It seems slower now that you're retreating, or maybe that's just your imagination's hope. You lean against one wood paneled wall, stroking your fingers down the robe's wide lapel, your other hand in a pocket, key heavy in your hand.

Your real life's never seemed further away than in this moment, and you can't begin to imagine going back to it again. A part of your brain is scheming – how can you manage to stay here? Bribery? Tricks?

The elevator door opens, revealing a short hall, all done in white and black. Statues of marble and onyx rest on pedestals of the same, atop black and white checker-style tiles. A white ceiling hangs over walls paneled in black, and to your right there is a very bright white door.

Turn to 174.

The night's not over – not yet.

You look at the open door of the elevator one last time and then turn your back on it – and a girl catches your eye with a smile. A minute ago she was probably holding a Greek amphora, but now she's naked except for bracelets at her ankles and wrists and a matching collar around her neck.

You smile back, and start to walk over to her – as satyr-man swoops in and picks her up. She laughs and he laughs and then you feel dismayed until she reaches out for you, one of her bracelets spinning on her wrist. You run to catch up with her, with both of them, stepping up into the painting, feeling the material of its construction give a little underneath your feet, like painted rubber. She leans down from his arms to kiss you, and you kiss her back hard, making both of them sway. You didn't mean to do that, to be so rough, but suddenly you're filled with need – you need to drain the dregs of your night here, and you know you don't want to be alone.

She surprises you, kissing you back just as fiercely, almost falling out of the man's arms. You run your hands up through her hair and then pull your head back, looking up at him, looking on, and it feels completely natural to kiss him too, so you lean up on your tip-toes to do so. The woman he's holding nuzzles against your exposed neck, and from behind and all around you, you can hear people joining, small cries of pleasure, louder moans, the sounds of flesh slapping flesh.

He sinks with her and you sink with him, and together you're all on one of the hillsides that wasn't really a hill after all. You kiss down his neck as your hands trail on her, and her hands are tugging his satyr costume down, and his hands are pushing your robe off. She spins and kisses your nearest breast while he rises to free himself from the suit's shaggy fur and kick it aside. You unloop your robe's belt to let it fall open and it flutters to the ground. The woman's hand finds your knee and begins to rise as your hand reaches for his cock over her and he's pressing fingers into your mouth to take your spit to use on her pussy.

Everything from your past that you brought with you somehow, through the entire course of the House and this extraordinary night, falls way. There's nothing left except touching and pleasure, finding her mouth with yours while he touches her there as your hand slides over his cock and her hands are on your breast and in your hair. You kiss her as he makes her moan and then you rise up to lean over him to take his cock into your mouth and feel him shake with need.

A hand falls on your back, you're not sure who's, and slides down, and parts your folds to find your clit. You rise up and look over your shoulder, and it's a woman you haven't met yet. She smiles shyly at you, and you give her a much more brave grin, before leaning back into her, and sucking cock again.

The woman you're leaning over writhes in time with his hand playing inside her. You pull back and look up and see him staring down, and you know that you're ready for more – then her mouth finds your breast and pins you there with pleasure.

He rocks back from both of you and moves down the hillside, spreading her legs apart with his – and then he takes you back from the woman who's been touching you, positioning you to straddle over the woman with her collar and bracelets. Her mouth is below yours, and you already know how sweet it is to kiss it, so you do, her tongue pressing in, your breasts dangling down, rubbing against her own, as she starts to move underneath you as he fucks her. You moan as she does, hungry and heated, and then feel him move behind you, grabbing your hips, to pull you onto his cock next. You cry out in pleased surprise at feeling him fill you, as the woman below you's hand reaches up to rub your clit. He takes you for three, five, ten strokes, thrusting so slowly you can feel every inch of his head and shaft, and then pulls out to fuck her again.

You moan, panting above her, trapped between them, and bend over to take and kiss her breast. There are sounds beside you now – the woman who touched you earlier is moaning as a man kneels, taking her from behind. Another man has slid himself between her legs and is eating her out while she gets fucked, and she has one hand on his cock, like she's trying to hang on. Her voice is rising as she's ridden, and you can tell she's getting close --

Fingers reach up and inside of you, calling your attention back – just as the satyr's cock slides in again. You moan, stretched anew, arching back into him – needing it more than you've ever needed it before. He holds onto your shoulders, pulling himself deep, and you look back, able to see the entire 'countryside' filled with throbbing groups of people, tangled in one another, voices beginning to take on urgent tones.

This time when he pulls out, it's not enough – you lean down and kiss the woman you're over, but crawl to one side – you need to be fucked immediately in a primal way. You lay on the hillside, panting with need, one hand on the slick space between your legs – when the orgasm of the woman who was touching you breaks through. Her voice echoes over the hill, moans vibrating up into a shout, until she's crouched over the man who was eating her pussy, gasping for air. He comes out from underneath her, kisses her hard, and she kisses him back – and then he looks over at you.

If he was anything before all this in a painting, it was a Greek god, and his erect cock does his divinity justice. You reach a hand out towards him just as the woman did to you, your key dangling down, and he crawls the short distance over to you, like an obedient beast.

He doesn't ask, because he knows he doesn't need to. He lays beside you, takes your jaw in his hand and pulls your head back to kiss you, lips wet from the other woman. Then he grabs your hips and pulls them back into his, his chest to your back. He takes your leg and slings it over his and enters your pussy from behind, in one smooth motion.

The cock that was almost being wasted earlier now fills you completely up. You moan and he growls in your ear and starts thrusting with purpose, pulling your hair away from your neck so that he can bite where it meets your shoulder, his hands helping to slide you on and off of him.

This was how you needed to be fucked. This was what you were missing earlier – what you may have been missing for your whole life.

No bullshit, no baggage, just unabashed need met with need – you spread your legs wider so that you can touch yourself as he speeds up.

Another woman steps into the portrait you're being fucked in – a dancing girl with dark skin, with gold jingling coins strapped around her waist and strung from clamps between her nipples. They make her chime as she walks up to you, kneels down, and puts her tongue where your hand is, to start lapping at your clit.

You moan helplessly, pinned by the Adonis's cock and the ministrations of her mouth. Her perfectly curved ass is too far away from you to grab or smack – but the chain dangling between her nipples is in reach. You take it and tug on it gently, and she groans while eating you.

A man who'd been dressed as a soldier earlier nears. There's a sword still slung at his naked hip, which matches the cock hanging between his legs. At seeing the three of you he reaches for himself – you get the feeling he's already spent himself once, but at the sight of the dancing girl's perfect ass he wants to go again. He kneels, taking her ass with both hands, and spreads her wide before pressing his mouth into her. You don't know where his tongue is going, but you can feel her shiver with pleasure against your clit and when he next rises up, his cock is hard. He slides it into her and you pull on her chain again and she moans, trapped between the two of you.

From beside you the braceleted woman's voice rises, as does the satyr still fucking her, her begging him to go faster and faster please oh please, and him grunting with each thrust as his hips and cock obey. Hearing their need, the sound of them unable to get enough, and the feel of tongue against your clit and the friction of the nameless cock thrusting inside of you -- you feel the kindling of your orgasm start to ignite. And with the soldier's thrusts pushing the dancing girl's tongue harder against you, and the Adonis's cock ramming home. It would be so easy to come now but you don't want to, you don't want to give up the night just yet –

The Adonis shudders, his hips arcing up into you, his cock stiff and his voice raw as he growls three times, shoving his load deep inside you. Your hand tightens on the dancing girl's chain until she stops and then you free yourself of him and her and look down and out at the room's ecstatically fucking occupants.

You rise up on your knees and cup your own breasts in each hand, pinching your own nipples, key dangling from your wrist, and demand, "More."

The occupants of the House obey their Mistress, and you are descended upon.

Men and women come, standing and kneeling, kissing and stroking, and you cannot keep track of who is touching you, nor do you want to anymore. You reach out with one hand and feel someone trail it down their stomach before sliding it into their pussy as another person's hand slides into yours. A man kisses you, pressing you back into the flesh that you asked for, your back leaning into another man's legs, his cock conveniently at mouth-height. You suck on him while someone dives down to suck at you and then you feel wet fingers slide into your ass, and the smooth hair of a woman waves across your chest as she bites your nipple, while another woman sucks your earlobe.

You're pulled, probed, kissed, sucked, searched. Your hands find mouths and necks and breasts and cocks, and your mouth is filled with ever changing delights, the warm heads of hot cocks and the sweet tang of soft pussy.

This is what it means to be Mistress of the House. To give yourself over to it, appreciatively – and to try to give as good as you get in return.

You could do this, stay in this space where everything is happening even as everything is still possible, for hours.

But the crowd parts, and a new Adonis is revealed, just as strong as the last, with dark curly hair and bright blue eyes and his cock is ready for you. He lays down on the hillside and as if by cosmic consent, the people that you're with guide you to his prone form and mount you astride him, facing out at the rest of the museum.

You pant over him, suddenly unaccustomed to just being in your own skin, without the warmth of others. And then you reach between your legs and settle him into the space where so many others have been before tonight – and yet still not enough.

He grunts and thrusts his hips up, riding his cock deep into you, and you're facing downhill so you're angled into his thrusts -- then the woman with the bracelets is at your side, kissing you, and your breasts, tongue urging you to come, and then the dancing woman with dark hair is there too and her hand is on your clit, and other mouths are on your shoulders and strange hands flow up your scalp and into your hair. You realize your orgasm isn't in your own hands anymore, it's in theirs, and you can feel it filling you up like bright white electricity.

Hands and mouths and pushing and thrusts and strokes and teeth and pushing and cock and thrusts and lips and more-more-more --

There's no way not to shout at the top of your lungs as you come, your wild voice joining the others all around you. You thrash with the force of it, your stomach going tight, and they catch you, as the man underneath you fucks himself home, his shout just as loud as yours. You spasm helplessly, your whole body shaking with the force of your orgasm, like you were just lightning struck. When it's finished with you the women carefully help you lay down onto the man's broad chest.

You feel in a very real way like you've just been reborn, covered in heat and having screamed so loud that your throat hurts. You slide off of the man and his magnificent cock to lay sweaty and spent by his side and he spoons you chastely, his breath rough in your ear, stroking one hand through your hair. Across the room other people continue to fuck, but you honestly don't know if you could manage it again. You turn and look up at him, and he at you, and he leans down as if to kiss you and you close your eyes.

And then the sound of a chime interrupts him. You can't help but count it, and when it strikes seven times, you have a sinking feeling you know what it means.

The man over you pulls his head up and smiles down at you, but shakes his head, softly, and you nod. Your magical night here as the Mistress of the House is through.

Across the room people groan and disengage, groups of six people become five, become two, as everyone gathers up their belongings – scarves, urns, swords -- and makes their way out. The women who were with you wave before trotting down the hill, and the satyr who first fucked you gives you a grinning bow. The man you were last with stands to collect your robe and holds it out for you.

You reluctantly stand and let him help you put it on. He kisses you on the cheek, takes a step back, and then walks down the hill.

You don't want to be the last person out, but you feel like you should be – this was your house, it is your right. And so you wait until everyone else leaves, and the elevator returns empty.

You step inside of it, and the doors close – you don't even have to use your key.

Turn to 173.

The elevator seems slower, or maybe that's just your imagination, hoping. You lean against one wood paneled wall, stroking your fingers down the robe's wide lapel, your other hand in a pocket, key heavy in your hand.

There's another bathroom, and another shower, and yet another robe. As the water runs, your real life's never seemed further away, and you can't begin to imagine going back to it again. A part of your brain is scheming – how can you manage to stay here? Bribery? Tricks?

The elevator door opens, revealing a short hall, all done in white and black. Statues of marble and onyx rest on pedestals of the same, atop black and white checker-style tiles. A white ceiling hangs over walls paneled in black, and to your right there is a very bright white door.

You don't want to go just yet, even though you know you must. You pause, and while you pause, you look to your left – where you can see the faint outline of a black door and its keyhole, flush with the black paneled wall.

Do you open the white door? If so, turn to 174.
Do you open the black door? If so, turn to 177.

ou turn towards the white door and lift your key up. The latch turns, the door opens, and you step inside.

The entire room's done in a tasteful shade of dove, or heather, or eggshell – off-white enough that it's not blinding even with the dawn's light coming in.

The butler's there, sitting behind a desk at the room's far end. You walk over to him, the end of the robe trailing like you're a queen.

He looks up from a stack of papers. "Mistress," he says with a kind smile, setting them aside.

"Butler," you acknowledge him. Out of all the people you've fucked tonight, he's the only one you've come to feel you know. It's good that he's here.

He stands and circles the desk, coming out to stand in front of you. "I'm afraid the night's come to an end. But I trust you've had a delightful time?"

You nod. "It wasn't how I thought it would be at all. But I'm very glad I came."

"As are we," he says, with just enough composure that you feel he's ignored the possible double-entendre you just made. You're a little sad that he has though, it's another small sign that your night is through. "There's a shower over here," he says, gesturing to one wall with an open door, "and we've brought you new clothing to ride back to the airport in. I suspect you'll be tired on the plane, I've packed you a pillow and mask."

You nod again. This is it. It really is almost all through.

"Am I," you begin slowly, building up steam – "Am I going to get to meet him?"

"Who?" the butler asks, tilting his head.

"The Master." You look around the room. There was a time when you wanted to ask silly questions like who was he, or why you, but – "I don't even want to have him explain all this anymore. I just want to meet him in person, to tell him thank you."

The butler folds one hand into his chest and bows. "I apologize. As the person organizing this event on your behalf, his night has been even longer than yours. I will tell him though. I know your thanks are sincere."

You nod yet again, and then look at the ground. "Then, there's just one more person left to thank here."

"Who?" he asks, eyebrows arched in curiosity.

"You."

"You have already thanked me enough," he says. You feel he means it, and yet – you reach out one hand. He takes it and brings it up to his lips.

If he was merely getting paid to do all of this, or if the House's spell broke with the rising sun, or if his Master held him to a certain set of rules – rejection now seems all too possible, perhaps even likely, and yet you still step in, taking what almost feels like your biggest chance of the entire night.

He looks up at you, eyes dark, weighing your intent, and then leans in too.

His hands find your robe's cord as his lips meet yours, and you're out of it in seconds, as he's guiding the both of you back to a couch. You feel it at the back of your calves and fall down onto it, him following you seconds later, catching himself on his hands.

Talking would ruin things, as would taking too much time. You're both in a race against departure tickets and reality, trying to capture one last piece of the night.

Your hands are on the waist of his suit pants and he's unbuttoning his shirt as you're undoing his belt, reaching in to free him, as he leans over, his open shirt fluttering over you as you open your legs to let him in.

His cock slides in and the both of you moan. And then he starts to fuck you, eyes on you, watching your reaction as he pushes deep inside. You reach one hand up to wind through his hair and the other down to rub yourself, arching your hips up to meet his, unable to look away from his hot brown eyes, wanting this moment, this feeling, this glamour to go on and on and on.

Your breath catches without you wanting it to. You feel your pussy taking hold of him, and he can't help but feel it too, he makes a soft moan, but doesn't slow or speed up, and you wonder if he wants to draw this out as badly as you know you do. He keeps stroking his full length in and out and your body moves with his, until it's like you're one person instead of two. Your muscles tense, your hips quiver, and you take one long last inhale like you're about to dive off of a high bridge, and instead of shouting like you've done all night, you come quietly in a series of long exhaling gasps. He lowers himself over you kissing you once hard, and thrusts and groans low, and you know his cum is pouring out inside. He lays over you for a second, breathing roughly, the stolen time between you all the sweeter for its quietness.

Over his back you can see the sunlight crawling further up the wall.

"I'd probably better be going now," you say, so he won't have to.

He lifts up, looking down at you again. "Yes, Mistress." He slides out of you and stands, tucking himself back in, zippering his pants and buckling his belt. You stand and decide to stay naked. After everything you've been through here, there's nothing left to be ashamed of. You walk towards the bathroom he indicated earlier, and he follows you.

You stand in the entrance. "Do I need to give this back?" you ask, holding up the key.

"It's yours to keep. As a memento of tonight."

You nod, hand on the door, and begin to close it, and he stops you.

"This is the only door here it cannot open again. This is good-bye, Mistress."

You lean out and kiss him on his cheek, before smiling bravely. "Good-bye, Butler," you say, and then close the door.

It locks behind you, sealing away the night for good. You inhale, exhale, step into the white marble shower, and turn the water on to let it run.

Turn to 249.

ou turn towards the black door and lift your key up. The latch turns, the door opens, and you step inside.

The entire room's done in dark tones, mahogany and merlot, and heavy blackout curtains are keeping out what you are sure would be the light of dawn.

The butler's there, sitting behind a desk at the room's far end. You walk over to him, the end of the robe trailing like you're a queen.

He looks up from a stack of papers. "Mistress," he says, setting them aside.

"Butler," you acknowledge him. Out of all the people you've fucked tonight, he's the only one you've come to feel you know, and you're happy that he's here.

He stands and circles the desk, coming out to stand in front of you. "I'm afraid the night's come to an end. But I trust you've had a delightful time?"

You nod. "It wasn't how I thought it would be at all. But I'm very glad I came," you say, intentionally.

"As are we," he says, with a light smirk, and then gestures. "There's a shower over here," he says, gesturing to one wall with an open door, "and we've brought you new clothing to ride back to the airport in. I suspect you'll be tired on the plane, I've packed you a pillow and mask."

It really is all coming to an end. It's hard to believe it, even though it's only been one night. You take a step towards the bathroom, then pause, looking back. "Am I going to get to meet him?"

"Who?" the butler asks, tilting his head, eyebrows raised.

"The Master." You look around the room, like he might be hiding it in it somewhere.

The butler folds one hand into his chest and bows. "I apologize. As the person organizing this event on your behalf, his night has been even longer than yours has."

You're not ready to leave yet – there has to be some way. You think hard, like someone who has sold her soul to the devil and is now looking for loopholes.

Your eyes scan his desk and see more of the ornate stationary, and you remember the Master's first note. "He said I had to bring him back his key."

The butler nods and puts his hand out. "If you give it to me, I'll take it to him."

"I'd rather give it to him myself."

He shakes his head sadly, returning to sit behind his desk. "He's not here right now, I'm afraid."

Looking at him in his extraordinarily fine suit, thinking about all the time you've spent with him inside the House -- realization lands hard.

"Oh yes he is," you say. "He's you – you're him." Your jaw drops in surprise, and you're not sure if you should hit him, or thank him, or both.

He sinks his head and shakes it, beginning to protest.

"Don't lie – not after last night," you tell him, and he looks up with a nod.

"All right. I am. You've caught me." He raises his ungloved hands in a gesture of surrender.

You circle the table to stand in front of him – now that he can finally answer all of your questions, it's hard to know where to begin. "Why – everything?" you say, voice rising, shaking your head in disbelief.

He smiles up at you kindly. "It pleases me to please you -- and I am a man of extraordinary tastes, along with extraordinary means. Do you really need to know more?"

"Yes!" You grin at him. "I want to know all about it! How you chose me, who all the rest of these people were – how big is this place, and – everything!"

He closes his mouth and shakes his head softly. "Everything takes too long," he says, his voice quiet. "And outside Mistress, it's already dawn."

You inhale, trying to think of some way to refute him, even when you know it's true, and you knew the rules coming in. Still – you're not ready to give up so easily just yet. You reach out to touch his cheek as he watches you. The look on his face makes you brave, and you lower your hand to his tie and undo its crisp knot.

Do you blindfold yourself with his tie? If so, flip to 180.

Do you gag yourself with his tie? If so, turn to 181.

ou pull his tie loose from around his neck. Taking it in between both of your hands you raise it to your head and tie it like a blindfold across your face.

"I don't know – I don't see any light in here," you say with a smirk, trying to seem cocky and brave, even as you're so nervous you could shake.

You hear him chuckle and stand, and you're afraid this is it, that everything's reached the end. Then you feel him move in, his body pressing close, his lips near your ear, and you hear him inhale, breathing you in.

He makes a thoughtful noise before saying, "Now that I've had time to reconsider – neither do I," and his strong arms pick you up.

You can't see where he's carrying you too – but you're already looking forward to what he'll do to you when you get there.

Turn to 249.

ou pull his tie loose from around his neck, and take it in between both of your hands and raise it to your face.

"I won't tell if you don't," you say, trying to sound cocksure before cinching it around your mouth and tasting the silk of a two hundred dollar tie. It's a scary ploy, going all in like this, gagging yourself in front of him – but it's worth it to see the surprised look on his face, before he can hide it with icy calmness again.

He makes a thoughtful noise and stands. Your heart starts racing, wondering what will come next, trying to prepare for disappointment while hoping for elation – and realize this is how it's been for you all night, the combination of fear and hope surging inside you, creating a high no drug could ever replicate.

He looks down at you, searching your eyes with his gaze. And then he takes up your hand with the key-bracelet, and you're afraid he's going to take it away from you and truly end the night.

The key dangles between you and he looks back at you, gagged, one last time.

"The House's Mistress always needs a safeword – and clearly you can't talk like that," he says, shaking his head in feigned exasperation at what you've done. "So this will have to do."

He takes the hanging key and swings it up. Instead of pulling the bracelet off of you, he carefully places the key inside the open palm of your hand and closes it into a fist. "If you release this then I'll stop," he says, "But not one second sooner."

The wolfish grin on his face makes his words a warning and a promise – and you're grinning back at him, behind the tie's loose gag. He reaches for your free hand and you gladly follow him further back into the House.

Turn to 249.

ou're hungry, but you'd rather let it build for now – you want to see them first. How often do you get to watch two beautiful women fuck, close enough to touch them? Not often enough.

You crawl over to be beside them, trying to force yourself to watch clinically but it's hard. Skin slides over skin, muscles moving below. Both of them have curves, and breasts, and they smell like shampoo and soap and woman. The kiss one another, first teasing, then hard, their hands vibrating between one another's thighs, like bees doing a honey-dance, and you can imagine their palms pressed against your clit and fingers pushed inside.

Kisses change to bites and moans, and the redhead pushes the black woman down. Her strawberry lips take their time, hovering over each breast in turn, breathing hot air over the darker woman's nipples, then blowing them cruelly cool. She licks both in turn, her whole mouth working, taking as much in as she can, sucking hard and deep, as the other woman plays her hands in the redhead's short hair, pulling it some, making the redhead purr.

You begin to feel, and not for the first time, that you're missing out. Your hips feel heavy and your clit starts to ache, but you're fascinated now, you want to watch through to the end of their show.

The redhead's face bows down between the darker woman's legs and she moans aloud. A hand disappears, and you know where those fingers are going, pressing inside to where she's hottest. The darker woman starts to move her hips and the redhead's mouth keeps time, and soon the she starts to moan.

It's an incredibly hot sound and it's hard not to kiss her neck when she does it. Even though you know you only want to watch there's something about watching her feel things that makes you want to feel them too.

She opens her eyes and sees you staring and you feel like you've been caught. Then she offers you her hand.

If you take it, turn to 184.

If not, go to 164.

*H*er breathing is fast as the redhead's tongue works, but she stretches her hand out again, and makes a come-closer motion with the first two fingers of it.

Sensing what she wants, even if you're afraid to ask for it, you move over and carefully lie down atop her stretched out hand.

You kiss her face because it's near now, and her lips touch yours at the same time her fingers graze your clit. You shudder, like you've been shocked – it was what you were expecting, and hoping for, and yet the fact that it actually happened – she starts to rub you and you moan, the sound muffled by her mouth.

You have a sudden urge to tear the black woman apart. You want to know her lips, her neck, her hair, her breasts, you want to feel them with your hands and taste them with your tongue, and you explore her body mercilessly, while the redhead continues to lap at her clit and pussy. Her hand follows you wherever you go, rewarding your curiosity with harder and faster strokes.

Everything about her is divine, her skin so soft stretched over muscles so smooth, with only an occasional hint of bone beneath. You want to taste every place on her, and discover her everything -- but her hand on you won't stop, even as her breath rises and catches, her moans more frequent now that you've been kissing her, rolling her hard nipples beneath your tongue. Your hips lower, desiring more, until you're pressing her hand against the bed and bucking into it, your mouth at the fullness of her breasts upon her ribcage as you grind yourself into her as she tries to stroke your orgasm out of you before she comes. Her voice rises again, almost into a scream, and it's knowing that she's near that does it, even more so than her vibrating hand, it's the sound of her about to release, feeling her hips shake the redhead's mouth and bed, there's no way that you can't follow her where she's about to go –

She shrieks and gasps, body writhing, translating the force of her orgasm down her hand and into you and pulling you over with her and then you're helplessly fucking her hand into the bed as you cry out over her. The moment you're done writhing she leans up and kisses you hard.

You fall beside her on the bed, breathing fast. You're not sure what you thought it would be like – but you didn't imagine it would be like this.

"Hmm?" she asks you, brushing a piece of hair back from your face.

"More," you whisper, back in charge.

She gives you a vulpine smile. "Of course."

Turn to page 186.

Or perhaps you turn your head and think you see a shadow inside one of the white fabric columns beside the bed. If so, turn to page 41.

"We can take this off, right?" the redhead asks, moving over to your side. They're both up now, naked, and you feel far too dressed. She puts her hands on your waist, and undoes your robe's loose tie. And then the darker woman's at your back, pulling your robe down, silk sliding against silk as your shoulders are exposed.

Hands start to brush you, and your own hands slide up. The darker woman moves your hair to kiss your neck as the redhead kisses at your lips. Your hand finds her waist, her back, her arm, her breast. She gasps as your fingers stroke the supple weight of her, rolling a thumb over her nipple as her tongue touches yours. The Black woman's hands were on your waist but now they're curling up your ribs, coming for your breasts, as she licks up to the spot behind your ear, making you shudder. She purrs as she starts to massage at you, one breast in each hand and the redhead rocks forward to rub her breasts on yours, and you bend down to take her nipple into your mouth, feeling it harden instantly. She gasps and brings her hands up to your hair, scratching fingernails along your scalp.

The fabric of the sheets and the softness of so much skin makes sliding easy. You press down to catch the redhead's other breast in your mouth while massaging the first one, and feel her move one leg between yours, and you willingly spread your legs open. Hands and fingernails trail down your back along your spine as the darker woman's breasts press up and then her hips move to grind against yours. You gasp, surprised at this more serious tone, but you like it, it's what you want too. You twist backwards to see her and catch her mouth with your own and moan into her as she starts moving her hips again against you. You move in time with her and find yourself grinding on the redhead's thigh. She purrs, and reaches a hand down, lowering herself bodily, until her face is at the level of your breasts and she can easily slide her hand in where her leg used to be. You know what she's going to do and yet you gasp as she does it – her fingers find your clit and start to rub.

The black woman bites your shoulder, and reaches through to

grab your breasts again, as though she's both holding you still and presenting you to be touched. The redhead kisses your nipples as her fingertips work their way back to your labia, sliding across them with your own wetness, before pushing one into you, feeling your warmth, making you moan.

"But – I –" you feel helpless, like you're not doing enough for them, even though you are definitely enjoying what they're doing to you.

"Shh. You're the Mistress," the darker woman says, absolving you of guilt.

"You can always pay us back later," the redheaded woman says, looking up. Then she bites at your nipple playfully and moves her hand more quickly.

The black woman lets go of you with one arm and sinks it down. You think she's going to touch herself – but instead, she touches you. She traces it down your spine until she reaches your ass and grabs it roughly, almost growling in your ear. You lift your leg because that's what you think she wants, and find it is – because her hand's now reaching at you from the back, middle and ring finger diving inside your pussy, rubbing her thumb against your asshole.

You gasp and moan at so much new sensation, as the redhead presses another finger inside, and it's like they're both pulling you apart. The redhead's using two hands now, one in you, and one on your clit, and she's still sucking on one of your breasts, rolling your nipple against her tongue, and the darker woman's licking and kissing on your back, with an occasional, unpredictable bite, and your hips start to wave, pinned by both of their desires for you to come between them, hard. You start to cry out as the tension builds, and the black woman bites you harder which turns you on more, and the redhead's fingers all speed up, and then you feel a thumb slide inside your ass, and the sensations are all too much – your breath hitches, again and again and your hips thrust and their hands follow and your orgasm coils inside you like a spring until it explodes out of you with a shout.

You thrash between them, helplessly, crying out as you do so, listening to their moans of satisfaction at you coming on either side.

You pant, exhausted even though you didn't put any effort in, and feel their hands slide out.

"Was that good, Mistress?" the redhead asks.

"Do you need to ask?" you say, reaching a hand out to run through her hair.

She smiles mischievously at you.

"Now," the woman behind you says, propping herself up on an arm. You twist to look back at her, and smile is positively wicked. "About paying us back….." She leans over the edge of the bed and pulls up two strap-ons from somewhere underneath it. "We have some ideas…."

Would you like to pay the black woman back first? If so, turn to page 27.

Would you like to pay the redhead back first? If so, turn to page 29.

ou stand and dry yourself off with one of the luxurious towels and pull your clothing back on, and head back to the hallway outside.

The same doors are there as before, as is the butler, waiting.

The conversation behind the purple door continues, but sounds more intimate. To open it, turn to 193.

The gray one still has the sound of rope rubbing over other rope. To open it, turn to page 54.

And walking down the hall you see a door you hadn't seen before – its color is eggshell blue, matching the sky of the nearest painting perfectly. If you want to listen at it, turn to page 190.

he butler follows you and watches you listen. You can't hear a thing. That might be frightening except for the fact that the door's the color of an expensively wrapped birthday present.

"What's inside here?" you ask him.

"Wonders," he says with a soft smile. "But I recommend you finish with all the other doors to your satisfaction first. Have you?"

You bite your lips, thinking.

The conversation behind the purple door continues, but sounds more intimate. To open it, turn to 193.

The gray one still has the sound of rope rubbing over other rope. To open it, turn to page 54.

If you want to return to the bath, turn to page 9.

But if you've finished the other doors and want to try your key in this one, go to page 125.

You pass a small bathroom on your way out, and take the opportunity to clean yourself up before dressing again. When you emerge into the hallway, it feels full of opportunity.

The same doors are there as before, as is the butler, waiting politely.

Would you like to return to the men behind the purple door? If so, turn to page 193.

There's still a bath being drawn behind the white door. If you'd like to visit it, turn to page 9.

The gray door still has the sound of rope rubbing over other rope, if turn to page 54.

And walking down the hall you see a door you hadn't seen before – its color is eggshell blue, matching the sky of the nearest painting perfectly. If you want to listen at it, turn to page 190.

The hallway feels full of opportunity now. The same doors are there as before, as is the butler, waiting politely.

Would you like to return to the men behind the purple door? If so, turn to page 193.

There's still a bath being drawn behind the white door. If you'd like to visit it, turn to page 9.

The gray door still has the sound of rope rubbing over other rope, if turn to page 54.

And walking down the hall you see a door you hadn't seen before – its color is eggshell blue, matching the sky of the nearest painting perfectly. If you want to listen at it, turn to page 190.

here are definitely people on the other side, talking. You knock politely before using your key to open the door. No matter what the butler's told you about the House and its servants, you don't feel right interrupting anyone.

You open the door slowly after that, and find that you're in an opulent bedroom, and that you're definitely not alone. There are two men lying in the purple bed that occupies the center of the room, and they look a little sheepish, as though you've caught them doing something, because you have. All of their hands are under the covers, and the satin sheets have ripples in suggestive places.

"Sorry," one apologizes a little breathlessly. He's young, his hair is blonde, and you can see his well-muscled shoulders. "We weren't sure –"

"Sometimes no one picks this door," the other says quickly. His skin is darker. He has a five o'clock shadow and as he rises up on one arm the sheet falls back, exposing his lean stomach.

"And it gets lonely?" you suggest, and they nod.

You know all about being lonely, lately. If given the choice, you do not want to feel alone again. But, key not withstanding, you also don't want to impose. "I didn't mean to interrupt – I can go –" you begin, making your way to step back through the open door.

"Wait –" the second man says, sitting up now, reaching a hand out to you. You pause.

Do you exit the room? If so, turn to page 194.

Do you walk over to the bed? If so, go to page 195.

ou turn around quickly and go back out into the hall, feeling a little flushed, and you find the butler, walking halfway down the stair.

"Not what you expected?" he asks solicitously, returning up to your floor.

"It's just – they're…there."

His lips lift into a grin. "They are indeed. And they only want to please you. It can be a heady and empowering experience, if you let it."

You look down at the key in your hand and wonder what's hiding behind all the other doors.

"You don't have to go back. Or you can choose another door entirely. Or we can stand here and make polite conversation all night. It's entirely up to you," he says.

You bite your lip in thought. Across from you both, there's a painting that stretches along most of the wall, with half-dressed satyrs and nymphs running wild, dancing in play.

And you realize that's what this could be, this whole night. It could be you, playing freely.

You set your shoulders and turn back towards the doors.

Do you return to the men in the purple chamber? Turn to page 195.

Or do you go through the white door, where the bath is still being drawn? Turn to page 9.

Or do you head directly to the gray door? Turn to page 54.

You still feel like you're walking in on them, but both of the men are smiling. The darker man is slightly nearer. "We didn't mean to scare you."

"You didn't," you assure him. You're curious, maybe a little wary, but not scared anymore.

"Good." The blonde man smiles at you now, drawing his legs up beneath him to kneel on the bed. He's naked, as is the darker man, you realize. You're jealous of them – you wish you could be so free.

"This bed is big and the night is long," the blonde man says. "Join us?"

"Unless you'd rather watch, that is," the darker man suggests with a slight leer.

If you would like to join them on the bed, turn to page 196.

If you would rather watch them, turn to page 215.

The blonde man leaves his hand out and you walk over to him. The bed is on a dais in the center of the room, you will have to step up onto it to join them, and somehow stepping onto it with clothing on does not feel right. In a moment you strip down and then you feel a little silly, standing naked in front of two strange men.

But they seem totally at ease with themselves which helps, and more importantly completely at ease with your nakedness. They look at you and from their erections you know they like what they see.

You slide down in between them because it feels natural. The darker man's lips find yours, his five-o-clock shadow tugging at your cheek, and his lips feel like they were meant to fit. The blonde's mouth finds your breast and you shiver, realizing that they're both touching you – and are going to keep touching you – at the same time.

The kiss deepens, as you wind your hand up into his slightly shaggy hair, and the blonde goes from kisses to gentle bites, his hand on your other breast, tweaking its nipple with his forefinger and thumb. A thigh slides up your thigh, and you're not sure whose it is, but you find that you don't really care. The blonde's cock is by your hand and so you take it, firm and smooth and warm, and you begin to stroke him, base to tip, as he moans.

The darker man kisses lower now, a trail down your neck, between your breasts, licking slowly down your stomach. The blonde keeps kissing at your breasts but is interrupted by the small moans he's making as you stroke him. You feel in control of him, and you pinch the tip of his cock lightly, making his breath hitch just as the darker man's mouth dips in between your open thighs.

You moan, teasing the blonde momentarily forgotten. The darker man's tongue licks gently at first, more breath than pressure, as he stretches his hands up your hips to feel what his actions make you do. You tilt towards him, and he drags his tongue's tip up across you, sliding back and forth against your clit with hot wet pressure. You shudder bodily, like a horse shaking off a fly, and then softly moan.

It doesn't take him long to discover what works best for you, and then he starts to tease you with that knowledge, doing exactly what you want, and then stopping, dark eyes looking up at you, gauging how long you can take before licking that certain spot again. It's like it's a game with him, and it's one that he's winning – one that you're ever so happy to lose.

The blonde keeps working on your nipples with his mouth, and you keep playing your hand up and down his cock when you can remember to – he thrusts softly against you, not trying to distract you from other pleasures, but unable to help himself in his need.

Your breath comes in hot waves as the darker man's tongue speeds up, his whole face pressed against you, using his beard to its full advantage as its roughness makes the nerves of your dripping pussy light up. Then he stops and pulls back, his breath as heavy as your own.

"Is there anything else we can do for you, Mistress?"

Do you tell him yes? If so, turn to page 198.

Do you tell him no, and keep going? Turn to page 210.

"Fuck me now," you say. Your voice sounds guttural to yourself and you don't mind. The darker man pushes himself up with his muscled arms, revealing the hard on that he's been lying on, the one that eating you out has given him. He kneels in between your legs and grabs your hips and pulls you down the bed to him.

You expect him to be rough, but he waits for a moment before entering you, as if to make sure you're ready – when you've never been as sure of anything other than this. The head of his cock dips inside you and his arms come up over your shoulders as he starts his first deep slide.

You're so wet, but you're still tight, or maybe it's the girth of him, spreading you wide. He holds himself over you, thrusting slowly, letting you feel all of him settle inside before pulling out slowly again. You begin to moan in time as he begins to speed up.

The blonde, who you'd forgotten in your haste to feel this full, moans at watching you get fucked. He's kneeling now and his cock is still hard, curved up against his washboard abs. The darker man slows and looks at the blonde and then looks meaningfully at you.

"Whatever you want, mistress, we'll do."

The dark man's cock feels so delicious inside of you, but it's hard not to be greedy when there's one more less than an arm's length away.

Do you take the blonde into your mouth? Turn to page 199.

Do you take the blonde into your ass? Turn to page 203.

Do you start jacking off the blonde as you get fucked? Turn to page 206.

Do you order the blonde to play with himself? Turn to page 208.

reedy maybe isn't the word for it – it's not strong enough. Your whole body is racked by need. The House has already been better to you than you thought it could be, why not push things a little more?

You rise up, letting the darker man's cock slide out of you with a moan. He looks at you, unsure, but you know you know what you want, and how you want it now.

You move to be on all fours, your ass facing the darker man, and you reach between your legs for him. His cock still slick with your own juices slides easily back inside of you. This new angle hits places that were not getting hit before, and you rock back and forth on him. He groans with each of your movements, but he stays stock still, perhaps afraid to disobey.

You stop moving and look over at the blonde, whose eyes are full of hope – and hunger. You reach out for his hips and pull him over until he's on his knees in front of you. The tip of his cock bobs as he tries to control himself. He thinks he knows what's coming, but he's scared to take your benevolence for granted. When you open up your lips and put them around the end of his cock, his patience and your kindness is rewarded with a desperate, ragged, breath.

The darker man chuckles, and then moans again, as you slide back on him, and off of the blonde's cock. They stay still, letting you decide who to favor. Should you press back and take the dark man deeper in, or lean forward to give the blonde more access to your mouth? You're in charge – for now. For as long as you want to be.

You look up and see the blonde looking down at you with earnest eyes, watching your mouth slide down his shaft, his head deep in your throat. He pushes your hair back not to take hold of your head, but to get a better view. Meanwhile the darker man's hands betray him on your next slide back. He clutches at your hips, trying to keep you pinned on him, so you can take all of him inside.

And you – you feel trapped, in the best possible way. They both want you and you want both of them. You feel full in a way you haven't felt before, and the radiating heat is intense. The man behind you starts gasping with each thrust, trying to feel more of you, while the blonde's need increases too, he wants more friction, and you're all too willing to give it to him, letting his cock slide in and out of your mouth roughly, him panting with each thrust. You reach your hand back between your legs and start to stroke your clit, which leaves you off balance, so every time your pussy gets rammed into from behind you almost fall forward, sliding further and further up the shaft of the blonde's cock as he moans. Now that you're touching yourself there's almost too much going on, too much sensation, a hand slaps your ass, and someone, you're no longer sure who, pulls your hair as they both try to ride you at opposite ends. Beneath your fingers a fire takes hold, and your stomach curves in, muscles taut. The darker man's cock follows you there, using the motion of his hips and hands around your waist to pull you further onto him. The blonde moves forward unwilling to be left behind and puts his silky firm cock in front of you so that you can't help but suck at it again. As though you were all in a circle instead, everyone is doing what they need to come, desperately relying on the others to need it more – you can tell the man who's fucking you is holding back now, barely, and in your mouth the blonde's cock is ripening, firm, hard, and strong. All they need now is what you need – to come.

You push against your clit frantically, willing it to open the door, to shove you into bliss, and after bone-crushing tightness, all your muscles taut, waiting, for release – it does, and the door is unlocked.

You thrash and moan, but the words are choked back by the cock in your mouth. Looking up you see the blonde looking down, reason vacant, everything he is, everything he wants to be, shoving into you. You feel the hot tang of his cum at the back of your throat as he cries out, holding onto your head carefully until he's done, and he pulls his cock out of your mouth with a breathless sigh, leaving waves of salty cum behind.

But you're not done yet. The man taking you from behind, now sure he is the only one, wraps you in his arms and pulls you back onto his cock, hard, your ass slapping against his thighs. He growls at your ear, and it's an animal sound for an animalistic fuck. He lifts you up with his strong arms again, and then slams you back down onto him. He's shuddering with need now and you hold his arms across your chest, relaxing into him, tilting your hips back. He slides you up and down himself, his cock finding places inside you that you didn't know were there, and then, with one final grab of your shoulders, pulling him all the way into you, does he let go with a beastial scream, riding against you in waves, his stomach and hips to yours, leaving his cock inside you until it is fully conquered. You feel his ragged breathing at the nape of your neck as he bends you both over, still shuddering, moaning low.

"Thank you, Mistress," he whispered in your ear, releasing you to sprawl upon the bed.

You lay languidly between the two men. You've never done anything quite like that before. Your mouth tastes like cum and there's hot fluids leaking out from between your legs.

Technically, you're dirty, perhaps in more ways than one, but as you catch your breath, it's hard not to feel like everything is glorious.

The darker man props himself up on his elbow. His other hand is stroking his cock as he looks at you appreciatively.

"Have we pleased you, Mistress?"

You almost laugh. "Do I look displeased?"

His lips lift in a perfect smirk. "No. Still, it's worth asking."

You close your eyes and roll back onto the mattress indulgently. "What's next?" you ask, still a little breathless.

The darker man smiles down at you. "It's up to you, Mistress. The entire house is yours."

You get the feeling you could come back to this room any time. But perhaps you should go and try out some others, first. You pick up your clothing, give them men an alluring smile, and move on.

You pick up your clothing and turn to 191.

*I*f you'd heard that two beautiful men wanted to serve you yesterday, you wouldn't have believed it. But now, after being here -- you sit up and scoot higher up the bed, pulling off of the darker man's cock, making him groan.

You look from one to the other of them, and smile a little wickedly.

"I'm sorry if you felt ignored," you tell the blonde.

He instantly shakes his head. "Not at all. We're only here to serve. If you're happy, then we're happy."

"That's nice to hear," you say, with a coy smile. "Stay right there." Then you look to the darker man. His lips part. He's still ready for you -- and you can tell by looking at him that he would like to continue.

"Mistress of the House," he says, waiting to hear what you decide.

"Come here," you command and, "Please," as an afterthought. You gesture for him to lay down by your side. He does as you tell him, laying down alongside you. You lift your leg up and settle it over his hip. His cock enters you again readily, fits into you like a hand meeting a glove, and you moan. It's hard not to just concentrate on this, it's easy to be distracted –

But you've been given a chance to live life to the fullest, at least for one night. And what could be more filling than….

You reach behind you, and find the blonde there, watching you, and you put a hand on his aching cock. Now that you know where it is, you take your hand to your mouth and lick it, getting it good and wet, distracted as you do so by the strong thorough thrusts of the darker man's cock. "Stop," you whisper on an upswing, and he does. You reach back with your wet hand to slick it along the blonde man's shaft. He moans as you touch him, and you twist back to see the look in his eyes. He wants in – in you.

You arch forward into the darker man, leveraging up your leg, exposing yourself to him. The blonde lays down behind you, his chest against your back, the head of his cock in the cleft of your ass.

"Slowly," you warn him.

"Mistress," he whispers in a gasp. The head of his cock finds your asshole and pushes gently against it. It's a strange feeling, but not bad, and slowly, inch by inch, he works his spit-wet cock inside of you. He lets out a guttural groan when he's shaft deep, and soon he's buried up until the hilt, they both are, in you.

You feel pulled, taut. Nerve endings have never sung these songs before, of raw pleasure and sheer decadence. And when they slowly begin to move again, it's almost overwhelming, the pressure of their bodies pressed up against you on either side. Hands everywhere, stroking skin, massaging breasts, cupping asses. When one slides out the other slides in, so it's like you're on a ride that doesn't have an end, they both feel good in such different ways, the confusion makes your head spin. And when the blond one reaches around to kiss the darker man as his hands find and begin to play with your clit, it's the final straw. The darker man kisses you next, as the blonde one fucks your ass harder, reaching in between all the skin and pressure to play against your folds, feeling the darker man's cock slide in and out of you and taking the wetness there to us to rub on you, onto your slick sweet spot, while with powerful groaning strokes he owns your ass. The darker man bites your nipple and starts fucking you just as hard. Their cocks are like pistons inside you, twinned to meet your pleasure, destined to keep fucking you until you give up all sense, all illusion of control.

You scream as sensations roll across your body, head to toe, there isn't a nerve fiber left in your body that was not part of your orgasm, you know because you spasmodically twitch again and again, the aftershocks of such intense pleasure unwilling to leave you.

The good thing is, they aren't done.

They dance with you groaning between them, ass and pussy tight, the friction they're building otherworldly, and the heat, the fire you thought was passed, was merely the first wave of what so much desire is capable of. The blonde is still rubbing your clit and the darker man's mouth is all over your breasts, cutting in with his stubble, and you're just holding on for dear life until the fire rages up again and consumes all of you. Everything is white for one pure sharp moment of ecstatic glory, and you hear the blonde cuss low, under his breath, and the darker man make a deliciously primal sound as he cries out loud. Inside of you, their cocks are pulsing, filling you back and front with cum. Your mouth is at the darker man's throat, tasting his sweat, as the blonde holds you, and all three of you stay there, pulled together for one last precious moment before exhaustion sets in and gravity pulls you apart.

You stay tangled with the men for what seems like an hour, as the part of you that soared off with pleasure slowly returns, and reality – or some version thereof – settles in. You move, and the key around your wrist is cool, and you remember that there are other doors. Kissing both men one final time, you stand up, pick up your clothing, and make your way out of the room.

Turn to page 191.

ou reach out for the blonde, and put your hand around his cock again. As your hand slides down his shaft, the darker man thrusts into you, and as your hand slides off, he pulls back out. You look up into his eyes and give him a playful look, which he returns with a wicked grin. He starts thrusting into you, long, slow, deep, and you mirror each one of his strokes on the blonde, head to hilt, smoothing fingers along his long shaft. The blonde's lips part and he moans, and precum starts to wet his tip. You run your fingers over it and use it to lubricate your hand.

The darker man's speed controls everything, keeps pressing into you, and then grinding up in a certain way that creates friction between him and your clit. You stroke the blonde with every move-ment the darker man makes, interpreting how it feels for you to him, speeding up, holding slightly tighter, as his pale hips start to buck, him trying to fuck your hand how you feel fucked. The darker man reaches down and takes a fistful of your hair so that you're watching him again, pulling tight enough so that he commands your full atten-tion, but you can't deny the blonde your hand, not when he needs to come as badly as you know you do. The darker man starts taking harder, faster strokes, knowing you're close, beginning to take what he needs to come from you. You stroke the blonde's cock frantically, trying to bring him off just as the dark man finds a final spot, his cock or his hips, pushing you up and over until your orgasm crashes over you, emanating out from your pussy in long, hot waves. He keeps going as you cry out, your tightness pulling him off inside of you as he thrusts wild, bucking into you with his need, before collapsing off to your side. Somehow you've kept stroking the blonde – and now you can give him the attention he craves. His gasps raise in volume until one final hip thrust forward through your precum-slicked hands takes him over the edge, shooting out hot pearlescent cum over the smooth skin of your stomach.

He crouches beside you, gasping. "Thank you, Mistress."

"You're very welcome," you say, stroking away the trail he left on your stomach, reaching over to him to smear it down his own chest.

You gather yourself slowly, enjoying the smell of sex in the air and the power you've had over the both of them. Then you dismount the bed and pick up your clothes.

Turn to page 191.

ou reach out for the darker man's hips and draw him to settle into you again. Then you turn towards the blonde.

"Touch yourself. Where I can see."

His eyes widen and his lips part. Kneeling where you can watch him, he settles one hand to his cock like a gunslinger reaching for a gun.

His hand plays up and down himself, as the darker man keeps fucking you. His cock drives deep inside, and he bends over to kiss your mouth, shoulders, neck, and through his shaggy hair you can see the blonde watching, touching himself, reacting to you two.

"Stroke yourself harder," you command. The darker man takes your hands and presses them over your head, each muscle on his stomach defined as he bends over you. He's taking you slowly now and you struggle, but he won't let you go. His eyes match yours for a second, and you know if you said the word, gave a new command, he would obey, but you don't want him to – you want the illusion of being trapped, fucked by one impossibly beautiful man while another of equal beauty watches, helpless, rapt.

"Harder," you whisper and the blonde's mouth opens wider, as precum starts to glisten at the tip of his cock.

The darker man keeps grinding into you, finding places inside you you're sure didn't exist before, and then he lets go of your hands to grab for your knees, pushing and pulling them up, spreading you wide. His thrusts become sharper now, and each stroke bottoms out inside of you, hitting the very back of your pussy. You lick your fingers and reach between your legs and start to rub your clit, as the dark man groans in pleasure and the blonde man starts to pant.

Sensation builds up, the awareness that choices have narrowed, that if you stay on this path then you most definitely will come. You look up at the dark man who is looking at you, and then at the place where his cock is sliding home, jaw dropped with fierce desire, and the blonde whose hand is stroking up and down his own cock so fast and hard. You're so close, just a touch or two away --

"Stop –" you command.

And everything does. The darker man makes an anguished sound, but he stops mid-thrust, and the blonde man bends forward like a drowned man finding land, hand still.

"Please, Mistress," the blonde begs with a gasp. "Please."

"Go," you say, like a perverted game of red-light green-light. "Go-go-go –"

The blonde cries out first, his free hand clutched in the sheets, jetting his hot cum in front of his knees, as the dark man starts thrusting again with need that cannot be denied. And your hand is on your clit and you rub and rub and rub that one spot until your hips swing up and your head swings back and you shout out, the dark man fucking you through it, fucking you into your orgasm, and out again the other side, until he is lost in you and his hips go wild, thrusting in the rhythm that they need for him to come as the waves of your receding orgasm roil through you.

The darker man holds himself over you, barely, like a gorgeous statue about to tumble down. You lean up to kiss him, and then kiss the blonde too, who's still gasping for breath off to one side. Then you slide back and look at the two men you've conquered, and wonder what else is left for you tonight.

You pick up your clothing, and turn to page 191.

he temptation to let him fuck you is tempting – you know from the look on his face that that's what he was hoping for. But right now is too divine, and maybe you're a little mad with power. There's nothing wrong with that though, is there? After all, the key wrapped around your wrist says the House is yours. He looks like he's enjoying himself – and you know you're enjoying yourself. It occurs to you that right now that's all that matters.

"No. Keep going."

He swipes his chin up the inside of your thigh, leaving a trail of your own juices on your skin, and then begins kissing and biting his way back down.

"Thank you," you breathe out, belatedly polite.

He chuckles in the back of his throat, a low noise, as his mouth meets you again. His lips part and his tongue returns, pressing hot circles underneath your hood, rubbing back and forth across your clit. He reaches one arm beneath himself and you feel fingers probing where his tongue was earlier, pushing easily inside your wet pussy. They press in a slow circle just as his tongue does your clit, feeling all the walls of you, making you stretch in a way that is so blissful it almost aches. The blonde's mouth finds your left breast, and his hand reaches across you to rub your right, keeping time with the darker man below. You moan and the darker man speeds up, eager to please you.

The blonde pauses to watch you both, purrs, and then kisses up your neck to suck on your ear. You wind your fingers into his hair and bring his mouth to yours, like you're biting into a peach. He hesitates, and you're surprised, until you see the mischievous look in his eyes. Instead of kissing you how you wanted to be kissed, he kisses you slowly, changing the kisses into bites, taking your lower lip between his teeth and pulling on it, like he wants to own a piece of you. He leans in for another kiss, and you feel his hot breath nearing, but then pulls back just at the moment you thought your lips would touch -- and then he does kiss you in that space that you're disappointed, surprising you.

You feel disoriented and lost in the best possible way. The darker man's mouth and fingers are driving you towards what you want, but the blonde is making you spin. You look down your own body for a second and see the darker man's eyes looking up between your thighs, as his fingers press deep, before closing again in concentration – and you realize that soft sound you've been hearing between heated breaths has been satin rubbing against satin as the darker man's hips stroke his cock against the bed.

The blonde looks down and sees what you see, and then leans for a conspiratorial whisper, and you whisper something back to him.

Do you tell him you want the darker man to fuck you now? Turn to 198.

Do you tell him to fuck the darker man? Turn to page 212.

Do you tell him to blow the darker man? Turn to page 217.

Do you tell him to keep going? Turn to page 232.

ou nod, and the blonde gives you another mischievous look, and quietly makes his way down the bed. The darker man's intent on your pussy, he wouldn't notice anyhow, but you move your hips more to provide a distraction. Everything he's doing feels amazing, but you're curious to discover what the blonde has in store.

The blonde strokes a hand down the darker man's back, and he shivers, pausing in eating you. He looks up again at you through your thighs, and you smile benevolently down at him, as the blonde strokes his back again while moving further down the bed. The blonde reaches the level of the darker man's knees and straddles them, his cock pointing up towards the head of the bed and you. The darker man's distracted by this and his hand slows inside you but his mouth doesn't stop.

The blonde massages his hands up the back of the darker man's thighs until he reaches his ass, and then keeps rubbing up, onto his back. Then he rubs back down and takes an ass cheek in each palm, and spreads the darker man's ass wide. This time the darker man's hand stops, and you feel his breath catch against your pussy, just as the blonde brings down his mouth.

Lips that were just kissing you are now eating out the darker man's ass. The dark man groans and his hips arch up, trying to give the blonde more access, while your own knees spread wide. He's being eaten out just as he eats you out, and the irony and the actuality are divine. The darker man starts panting, translating his own pleasure into something you can share. You moan, look down at both of them working with abandon, and wonder what you've wrought. The darker man's hand position changes and he starts making a come-hither motion inside of you – and you see the blonde's hand come up, pressing fingers into the darker man's wet ass. The darker man grunts as you groan and the sounds continue as hands work fast – and then the blonde rises up again. He takes two kneeling steps forward and – eyes on you – leans forward, dipping his cock down to touch the darker man's ass. The darker man's breathing speeds up and his hand fucks you as frantically as he wants to be fucked. You watch the blonde's cock dive in, ever so slow, and the darker man groans, the sound muffled by your pussy. His fingers and his tongue were already bringing you to the point of no return, but watching him get fucked adds another dimension entirely. The blonde pulls out slowly, his hands holding on to the darker man's hips, and the darker man translates this into you, sucking and pulling his fingers out – only to press in again, hand and tongue, as the blonde strokes back in with a groan, riding the darker man's ass into the bed.

The blonde's cock sets the pace and he starts to speed up. He drives his hips forward, pinning the darker man down, who in turn puts another finger inside of you, and then a third, so that you're stretched wider with each translated stroke. Your hips begin to buck at his mouth, as the blonde rams into his ass, grunting each time his cock lands home. The darker man looks up into your eyes and you see the lost look there like you had earlier, almost as if he's being used up, and then he groans again into you and you know he doesn't mind. The blonde leans down closer now, you can see his stomach muscles curve and tense, driving both of their hips into the bed with each hungry thrust, and the tip of the darker man's tongue finds that one bright spot on your clit and rubs it into a flame, until no matter where he licks it feels just right. The blonde starts to go faster, sweat dripping down onto the darker man's back, and the darker man is sucking you, licking you frantically, the groans he makes with each thrust coming so often they're a continual moan. The blonde pounds him harder, sending shudders through you both, grunting as the darker man's ass takes his cock in to the hilt, balls slapping with each stroke, and you feel the walls of your pussy begin to clamp down on the fingers pulling inside of it. You reach down and grab the darker man's hair because you need to ride his tongue home.

The moment stretches out forever, tongue on clit, fingers shoved deep, ass arching and cock ramming, together the three of you are like some infernal machine designed to fuck. The darker man's fingers curl forward again as his tongue drags across and it's like he's pulling an orgasm out of you, you begin to come and you don't stop coming, your hips thrash and you scream. The blonde fucks him relentlessly, making the bed shake, so that you don't know which shudders are yours and which are his as the orgasm flows out of you and into him – his hands clench the sheets on either side of your hips like he can drag it to him and take it for himself – and then he jerks wildly, his hips acting of their own accord, spasming his load into the darker man's ass, and the darker man's hips rise to take more of him in, as if such a thing were possible, and then grinds his hips into the bed before doing it all again, his ass greased with the blonde's cum, using the last of the blonde's erection and the slickness of the sheets beneath the three of you to finally get himself off, thrusting his hard-on into the bed until he too can be satisfied, with a final deep groan.

Your thighs are slick with your own juices and his spit. The darker man crawls up the bed towards you like a shipwreck survivor and you know he's leaving a spreading wet spot of his own. The blonde throws himself down on your other side still breathing raggedly.

Under any other circumstances in the world, sleeping here with them would be the finest course of action.

But there's still a key dangling from your wrist and many other doors....

Pick up your clothing and turn to page 191.

"Are you sure?" the blonde man says. "You can join in any time."

You nod – and wonder if they're going to do what they do with the sheets on, and if so, could you order them to take them off? The key dangles from your bracelet, tapping lightly against your palm.

The bed is up on a dais and there's other furniture in the room. Wooden tables along the walls hold antique figurines. Primitive clay figurines penetrate one another, next to ecstatic orgies carved in stone. The faces time has not worn smooth are smiling back at you, frozen in bliss.

And there's a chair not far from the front of the bed. It was meant for watching, you realize. You sit down and its deep upholstery eases around you, taking you in, giving you a front row seat.

The sheet that covered the men has slipped away. They're kissing one another as their hands stroke up and down firm chests and smooth stomachs, and you can see every inch of their exposed bodies. Both of them already have hard-ons, cocks curving forward, eager to be used.

They take turns casting you looks – not because they're nervous about being watched, you realize, but because it turns them on. They want you to see them as they kiss, as the blonde begins to go slowly lower on the darker man's chest, kissing between his nipples down to the dark line of hair on his stomach, at the end of which waits his erection. The darker man moans as the blonde's mouth gets nearer and then gasps as lips touch his firm shaft. The blonde moans at that, at the power he now holds over the other man, and your own lips part, a little breathless, like you might moan too.

The blonde slides his lips up the darker man's shaft and they find a rhythm in front of you. The darker man holds onto one of the posts of the bed and rocks forward as the blonde rocks back, always trying to keep more of himself in the other man's mouth. And when the blonde comes forward and buries his face, taking his cock deep, the darker man lets out guttural groans.

Watching other people fuck is a primal thing, and your body aches at being left out. The empty space between your legs begins to throb.

Do you touch yourself? If so, turn to page 234.

Or do you keep watching? If so, turn to page 236.

You nod, and the blonde gives you another mischievous look, quietly making his way down the bed. The darker man's intent on your pussy, he wouldn't notice anyhow, but you move your hips more to provide a distraction. Everything he's doing feels amazing, but you're curious to discover what the blonde has in store.

The blonde strokes a hand down the darker man's back, and he shivers, pausing in eating you, and looks up. You want to come, and he is pleasing you – but the key dangling from your wrist makes you in charge of him, doesn't it? And right now you're feeling royally benevolent. You smile down at him, just short of a leer.

As you do so, the strong muscles of the blonde's arm start to move. You can hear the sound of skin sliding against satin, and watch the dawning realization of the darker man as he realizes just what you've granted him. He may not be able to fuck you with his hard on, but there's no need for it to go to waste. His mouth opens as the other man grasps him and starts stroking.

"Mistress –" he whispers.

You spread your knees slightly wider in response – and he gladly dives back down. You reach down and spread yourself wide for him, so that his tongue can find every part of you, the tightness of your skin making each of his touches, tongue and hand, more profound. Your hips start to arch up into his mouth of their own accord – the only thing that keeps you pinned is his hand, which has stopped spinning and started sliding in and out of you, his fingers surely mimicking the blonde's hidden hand, as his hips start to thrust into the bed of their own accord.

It's hard not to watch the tableau taking place below you, watching yourself get eaten, watching the blonde intent on working the darker man's cock. The blonde takes his free hand and sucks on his first two fingers, and then positions them on the cleft of the darker man's ass, pressing for a moment, before disappearing inside.

The darker man groans low, pinned between the blonde's hands. His hips jerk spasmodically, wanting to feel more of everything, finger-full and cock-held. For a second you're forgotten, but watching him is hot – until his eyes lock onto yours, hungrily. His hand inside you starts again, and his other hand darts in, spreading you wider than you already were, then maybe you thought you could be, before pulling back out and putting his wet finger on your own ass and he looks up to you for permission.

Do you nod and let him slide fingers into your ass? Turn to page 219.

Do you shake your head no? Flip to page 223.

*Y*ou nod, but he won't go in – he rubs you there instead, massaging you until you know you're ready, until you're almost begging for him, crouching up above you like a cat. You've forgotten his mouth and your pussy, you can't concentrate on any other feeling while you're waiting for him to enter you, not knowing when it will happen, only sure of how good it will be. He starts to slip inside you and you pant, as your own juices grease his way in, your ass tighter than your pussy or your mouth, feeling every inch of the finger he's pressing inside. He pushes in to the knuckle, and then pulls back slow.

The blonde's stopped now, watching both of you, mouth wide, breathing rough. As the darker man's finger slides back inside, slow, ever so slow, you know whatever pretense of control you had has been lost, because you'd do anything to make him keep going now. And just as you think the sensations cannot get any more exquisite, he pushes a second finger into you to explore.

The blonde starts again, and you can see his hand working between the darker man's thighs, and hear the sound of his hand slapping the other man's ass as he penetrates him just like you. Your hips arch up and then back, meeting the darker man's hand, starting to work it as you would a cock, and at this he leans down, hungrily, back over you. His mouth finds your pussy again as you rise, and licks you voraciously, then lets you go as you fall – you could stay high, being eaten, but then you'd lose the sensation of him sliding in and out. It's a rough choice, but if you go fast enough, you might not actually have to make it – you start to twitch faster, using him to fuck yourself as the blonde keeps fucking him. The darker man moans every time the blonde's fingers go deep, just as his hand plants into you, and you still hold your pussy wide so that each time his mouth meets it you can slide all of yourself down his soft tongue and rough chin.

Instinct takes over and thought is lost – it's your turn to spasm, your hips acting on their own, your body doing what it needs to, to fuck and get fucked. You speed up, taking his fingers faster, rubbing yourself harder against him, as the blonde's hands work him front and back. You forget anything you ever were afraid of, and want to take whatever it is you want from the world, as long as it means getting this – and the darker man leans over and down, pinning your hips down, fucking you as hard with his hand as he is with his face, his tongue, his chin – you scream and your hips buck and he follows you, tongue thrashing against your clit, fingers sliding in and out of you fast enough to start a fire. You scream again and it ends in a hitch in your throat as the orgasm waves through you, head to toe, your hips dropping, arching, then dropping again, and finally he relents, but only after licking you, pussy to clit, one last time.

Then he crouches over you, hands and knees, finally giving the blonde full access to his cock and his ass, and the blonde takes it. Concentration makes his face fierce as he keeps ramming his fingers into the darker man's ass, and the darker man arches back like a cat, grunting with each stroke. The darker man's cock is waving over you, forgotten by the blonde momentarily – and then you reach out through your legs and grab it.

The man who just made you feel like that surely deserves the same. You play your hand up to the head of his cock and squeeze it gently, teasing it and him, and his jaw drops at your touch. The blonde, seeing you take charge below, rises up to knee behind the darker man, his own cock hard. He takes one stroke down the sweat of the darker man's ass, then enters in, as the darker man groans.

Now the darker man's getting fucked on top of you, as you stroke his silky cock with your hand. They cry out with each thrust, and you stroke him firmly, hilt to head and back again with one hand, while reaching back between your legs with the other. Their sweat mingles, dripping down on top of you as they sway, pinned and pinner, and you can see the blonde's jaw tense with each deep row he makes into the darker man's ass. The darker man sways forward with each stroke, running his cock harder and harder through your hand, while your other hand rubs at the spot he just licked, rekindling the flame he left behind.

It doesn't take long to feel another urge build inside of you, with them writhing on top of you like this, like sculptures from ancient times come to life. The darker man's hands are by your shoulders and he's panting, his stomach curving forward into your hand with each of the blonde's thrusts. He bends to look down at his cock and your hand and then he leans down to kiss your breast and bite at your nipple in hunger and you squeak because it's new and surprising but it feels good, and he growls and does it again. Your fingers work faster, on yourself and on his cock, and everything's wet because you've reached down to take your own juices and use them to lubricate your cock-stroking hand. With a final frantic pulse, tapping your own clit in a code only you truly know, you bring yourself up and over again, arching forward, stomach stiff as a board, curling up under the darker man who is still getting fucked, hard. You cry out, writhing beneath their show, and they groan in guttural response.

The blonde's barely steadying himself on the darker man's shoulders now. You reach up with one wet hand to touch the darker man's shaft and then stroke down to his heavy swaying balls – and then scoot down the bed between their legs to touch the blonde's balls too. He groans at your touch, and they're heavy in your hands but you can feel them tighten, lifting, and you know they're getting ready to shoot their load. With your front row seat to their fucking you stroke both of their sacks. They moan and purr in turns, which makes you bolder – you quickly lick a finger and reach up to push it into the blonde's ass. He grunts loudly and you feel it ratchet tight around you, finding a hard hot spot to rub inside, playing him like you were played before. His groans lower and becomes more rough until his fingers clutch at the darker man's shoulders. He plows in and in and in until he comes with a shout, cock shoved deep inside the darker man.

The darker man reaches down now, desperate to come, and grabs his own cock as you reach for his balls, stroking them, sending shudders through him as the blonde spends the last of his erection thudding through. The darker man's breath rises in pitch and volume, speeding up as his hand does, and his balls lift too, high and tight, coming to the edge, and then his hips spasm forward and contact is lost as he jerks over you, warm cum streaming down like silver ribbon, as he lets out an anguished cry. He gasps over you, unable to catch his breath, and the blonde moves back, falling to the bed. The darker man looks down at you, his cum spattered over your stomach and breasts, both of your chests heaving.

"Thank you, Mistress," he says, when he can speak again.

"You're very welcome," you say, the soul of polite. You clean yourself up with the sheet, and then reach for your clothing.

As hot as this room is, there are still other doors.

Flip to page 191.

ou shake your head subtly. You're not ready for that, not now, not when his mouth needs to be on your clit. He pauses, then gets a wicked grin, and reaches up to spread your knees even wider, and redoubles his efforts again.

The blonde is working him front and back, but the darker man only has a mouth for you – his tongue is using your clit hard, sliding up and down, and then side to side. You don't know what he'll do next, and so everything keeps being a surprise. He growls into your pussy, and starts shaking his head like he's trying to take all of you in, while the blonde keeps fucking his ass and stroking his cock, making the darker man's hips jerk, harder, and you wonder what you missed in deciding not to be beneath them when he raises up and looks back at the blonde.

A look passes between them – you're not sure what – but then the blonde is laying down and the darker man is moving to straddle him. Then he grabs your hips and brings you closer to him on the bed.

His hands cup your ass and raise your pussy higher as the blonde takes his cock into both hands, and the tip into his mouth, and you see what's going on now. He's going to fuck the blonde's mouth just as his mouth is fucking you.

You may not have let his cock fuck you, but he's still going to take what he wants.

His hips thrust with purpose now as he growls again, tongue wild on you, fingers pressing further in, a third finger, then a fourth, his hand spreading you, again and again, using the same rhythm that he's using to fuck the blonde's mouth, and you can hear the wet sounds from both activities as he builds speed up. You reach up to stroke your own breasts and pull at your nipples, the friction creating even more electricity. The darker man's strong hands lever your ass up and down, like he's licking the last morsel off a plate and then he goes still. You gasp in frustration and look down and realize the blonde's started licking his balls – and the darker man's started panting in need.

"Mistress," he says, half-apology, half-pleading.

You reach a hand down run it through his hair. His mouth and chin are covered with your juices. You can wait for another minute – from the look on his face you know it won't be long.

"Fuck him," you say, permission and a command. The darker man cries out and crouched on his arms above you starts fucking the blonde's mouth with more purpose and intensity. He hisses out as the blonde's mouth takes him deep, and the blonde moves his hand, letting all of the darker man's cock slide in, until his face is buried in short-trimmed pubic hair. The blonde wraps his arms around the darker man's thighs, following his cock as it rises back up.

The darker man groans and starts thrusting in earnest, his hips rocking into the blonde's face. Watching him get eaten is hot – you push your other hand between your legs to start up where his tongue left off, and soon your hand in his hair starts to clench involuntarily, like you're holding onto a rein. He moans at this addition of light pain.

"I told you to fuck him," you say with fake anger. Sweat is dripping down his back and onto your thighs. The blonde's groaning with each thrust, the darker man's cock dominating his mouth.

"I am –" the darker man gasps out.

"Harder," you command. You start rubbing yourself and your clit feels sharp and alive, and your other hand pulls his hair tight. "Harder," you say again, talking to him, your hand, yourself.

The bed's rocking beneath you, you have no idea how the blonde's mouth is surviving his thrusts, but he's so close to coming and you want to make him come – "Harder, harder, harder," you whisper with each stroke of his hips, rising in tone and volume and speed. "Harder – harder -- harder – please –"

"Oh God –" he gasps out and then he shouts and his body spasms. His hips drive down again and again and you know that the blonde's mouth is full of hot, salty, sweet.

You feel smug, and pull the darker man's hair one last time and then release it, scratching sudden fingernails up his scalp, making him purr and shiver. Your other hand slowly circles your clit, relishing this in-between moment, keeping yourself turned on, feeling languid and hot. The blonde rises up, covered in sweat, his almost bruised lips grinning wickedly.

That's when you realize they're both watching you touch yourself. You start to close your knees, but it's too late – the darker man presses your leg down and starts sliding a hand up your thigh, and the blonde's doing the same on the other side. Their faces are intent with concentration as they watch their fingers penetrate you simultaneously and then you're so glad you didn't hide.

Four fingers play inside you, two from each of them, and they're pressing and pulling, you can feel them both stroking the inside of your walls, moving at different angles and different rates, touching spots that you'd swear have never been touched before. Your pussy feels so tight, stretched wide, and your clit's turned into a button that you can't help but push. You lick your hand and use more fingers so that there's no way not to stroke yourself, as they stroke into you. Your hips arc of their own accord, dancing with their hands, but no matter how you move they have you pinned, and the pleasure of being full verging almost into pain and then back again. The blonde's cock is hard, curved up against his stomach, and the darker man's erection is returning, no matter that he just came. But no cock could fill you quite like this, their movements firm and wild and unpredictable until you run your fingers over your clit like you're strumming a guitar and you know the next chord is going to bring you off – your hips thrash and you curl up, your orgasm lifting you off the bed as the muscles in your stomach move in waves, your whole body conspiring to somehow take them in. They groan in satisfaction just as you do, but their hands don't stop until you're through, and you lay breathless on the bed.

The darker man sinks beside you, his breath warm beside your cheek. He smells like your pussy and you're tempted to kiss him to taste yourself. The blonde is lying on one elbow, stroking his cock lightly, like an afterthought.

"Mistress..." the darker man says and leans in to whispers suggestions in your ear.

Do you give the blonde a blow job? Turn to page 227.

Do you jerk the blonde off? Flip to page 230.

Or do you pick up your clothes, and decide to visit other doors? If so, go to page 191.

$\mathcal{I}$t's impossible to be stealthy on satin but you try. You sit up and rock up onto your knees and act like you've decided to crawl off the bed, gorgeous men forgotten. You can feel the blonde watching you, knowing that you're the reason he's still playing with his cock, and you wonder if he's working up the courage to ask for what he needs.

Just as he inhales to speak you turn on him and rise up. You put one hand on his shoulder and push him down, so that his erection is the highest point on his body. He gasps, beginning to hope.

You situate yourself between his legs so that you can look up at him. He's sweaty but it smells good, and the reverent look on his face as he looks down at you, eyes intent, mouth open as if he's about to say a prayer, is hot. He needs you – his cock needs you. You tilt your head down to take the head of his cock into your mouth, and he groans.

He's already been hard for who knows how long, you lost track of time long ago, all you know is that he hasn't come yet. You kiss the firm-soft head of him, taking it and only it into your mouth, teasing him as you leave his shaft alone. His hips thrust up, trying to get you take more of him, but you pull back entirely, and then just breathe down him, leaving a trail of warm soft breath against his shaft. He moans again, and you take hold of him with one hand, slowly sliding it up and down, watching him. It's torture, but he won't tell you so – he doesn't need to, you can read it in the way his body moves, his hips arcing and his hands grabbing into the sheets. You lower your head again and in an act of benevolence, take him all in, all at once, his cock sliding deep into the back of your throat, making him moan.

You start to work on him with your mouth and hands, stroking, sucking, as his cock gets even harder – when you're startled by a change.

You'd been so busy concentrating on the blonde that you'd forgotten the darker man – and he's sliding himself face up between your legs below.

Now you know how he felt earlier, distracted, as he grabs hold of your hips and pulls them down so that he can lap at your clit again. Sensitive after your first time coming, this new attention sends lightning bolts through you. The blonde writhes forward, grasping at your breasts, pinching your nipples, desperate to get your attention back on him – and you do so, taking his cock into your mouth fully again as you let go of your hips and start to pulse.

The blonde's thrusting and the darker man's lapping and fingers are pushing inside of you again. The blonde runs fingers through your hair, as you hold yourself over his thrashing hips, letting him fuck your mouth with abandon, grinding your clit down into the darker man's mouth, his tongue on you and in you, and you curling down trying to get more contact with his face – you're hunched over both of them, the blonde's cock is getting harder in your mouth just as you feel your pussy start to go tight –

"Mistress –" the blonde gasps and you know he's asking for permission to come. To answer him you reach up and cup his balls, stroking them towards you, and he screams out, his hands holding your head in place while he thrusts. Cum explodes into your mouth like you've bitten into a ripe pear, and his cock bobs like the living thing it is, shooting his full load.

You rise up off of him and see the helpless look he's giving you as he looks down, still worried that somehow in his need he's gone too far, but you swallow, and let him watch you lick the last of the stickiness off your lips, and he groans anew.

The darker man's tongue isn't forgotten. Now that you're done getting the blonde off, you crouch on all fours, settling deeper in. The blonde crosses the bed back to you and starts kissing you desperately, hands stroking over your breasts, pulling at your nipples, his mouth and teeth hot at your ear and neck. His mouth makes its way down to your breasts and sucks at them hard, biting your nipples while the darker man's tongue flicks your clit, and it's like there's an invisible line between the two places, stretched tight. You groan and he bites again, one sharp burst of pain forgotten the second it's replaced by hotter need. The darker man below you turns his head and nips at your inner thigh and you groan again as he returns to your clit, fresh pain hovering just below the pleasure line. The biting and pinches continue and you feel like they're going to eat all of you up – and if they did you wouldn't mind. You're trapped there between the two of them, kneeling, knees wide, your orgasm forming inside of you like a new sun, ready to explode –

You don't know what pushes you over, teeth, tongue, a pinch, there's too much going on to differentiate anymore – but something does, opening you and letting waves of pleasure explode out. You crouch forward holding onto the bed with your hands, while the darker man's mouth follows you and the blonde keeps biting and pulling, you make animalistic noises. This orgasm is deeper than the last one, it's taking more out of you to come -- you drive your hips down once, twice, like you own the darker man's mouth, and he groans in return, still licking you as you ride him.

With a final gasp the pleasure leaves you, wrung out and exhausted. You collapse forward onto the bed, the blonde falling at your side. The darker man crawls up to join you, and you kiss him, not caring that he tastes like you.

After a time you remember that the night has to end eventually – and you've still got more doors to open. Pick up your clothing and turn to page 191.

he blonde is beautiful in half repose against a pile of pillows, playing his hand up and down his cock. It's mesmerizing to watch him stroke himself – and now that he knows he's being watched he's going faster.

You crawl down to join him while he watches you move. "Want some help?" you ask him with a knowing grin.

"Of course," he says, and swallows.

You watch his hand as if you were a scientist for a moment, and then swat it aside, taking control of his erection yourself. You slide down it and back up again experimentally, his silky skin soft over the hardness of his cock. You take a few strokes, up and down, exploring all of him, from his head to his hilt, as his breathing starts to speed up.

You decide to go in the same rhythm as his breath, each inhalation and exhalation equaling one full stroke. You like having this power over him and are mystified that men are sometimes so easy to control. Sometimes it seems like you can hold just this one part of them, and you can lead them around for the rest of their life. His breathing speeds up again, and you don't want to hurt him, so you take your hand back and spit into it to lubricate things some. He gasps as you release him, and then groans at seeing you spit, knowing what will happen next.

It's easier to go faster now, and faster's what he needs, he's started grunting each time your hand slides to his hilt. The key around your wrist slaps against his stomach with each stroke.

The bed moves unexpectedly, and you look up. The darker man's shifted and he's started playing with his own softer cock, turned on by watching you but recently spent. And you have what you think is a marvelous idea – and glance meaningfully to your other side.

The darker man quickly moves to where you've looked, and you put a hand out for him. The blonde looks over and up to see, and then realizes your plan and chuckles low. You start all over again with him, slow, your other hand on the darker man's cock.

It doesn't take long for him to become hard again under your ministrations, especially with the blonde's groans of pleasure encouraging him to catch up. His cock's slightly wider than the blonde's, but the blonde's is longer, and so no two strokes on either man are the same. You lick your hands again and both cocks are hot under your newly cooled palms.

It's easy to do what you want with both of them. Clear drops of precum start to show on the blonde, and you use these to further slick your hand, but you don't want him to come first – you want to make both of them come for you at the same time. You close your hand on the head of his cock a bit, tamping him off, while you stroke the darker man liberally. His cock is close to catching up, you can feel it strain inside your grip like a python, getting hotter as more blood rushes in. He groans and his sounds match the blonde's from a moment ago, and you know both of them are begging for release.

You stroke them both firm, and long, and with abandon, from the tips of their heads, with precum drooling out, to their bases where their cocks meet their curved and muscled stomachs. Their hips start to pound up at your hands in a mated rhythm, one than the other, until you're not stroking them anymore, it's all you can do to hold on.

The blonde releases first with a shout, milky fluids shooting out, the darker man just half a second behind, his silvery flow in high contrast against his skin. Both of them pulse again, now out of time, the final waves of pleasure spilling on their abdomens. You sit up, both men conquered, and delicately wipe your hands off on the sheets.

You hate to leave them – but other doors await. You dismount the bed with a smile and pick your clothes up off the floor.

Turn to page 191.

ou smile but shake your head. Right now this is all about you – and you're starting to breathe faster. The darker man's hand inside of you changes position and starts making a come-hither motion, fingertips pressing against the inside of your pussy, like he's going to pull an orgasm out of you, and you realize he just might if he keeps doing that like that like that -- your hips start to twitch as the blonde purrs by your side. He leans down to kiss your breasts, leaving a trail of cooling heat behind him, and your nipples become hard and tight.

The darker man's mouth sucks at your clit while his fingers work inside. He's rubbing places a cock could never reach on you, so hard and in and up. It's almost too much to take, too much sensation, it almost feels too good. You moan and he moans too, he knows the effect he's having on you and is loving taking control as fast as you can lose it.

You start to rock in time with his hand, pulling down as it comes up, so that it presses harder inside your pussy. His mouth fights to stay on you as his hand follows you up and down, his hand inside cocking you like a gun, ready to be released, the pressure is almost pain but it feels so-so-so very good – you gasp and shudder and then cry out loud, riding his mouth and hand, as waves of fluid pour out of you with your orgasm, a visual representation of your pleasure, like somewhere deep inside a champagne bottle's been uncorked. You saturate the bed with moist heat, your hips dropping moments after your final thrust.

The darker man chuckles as though making you squirt was his plan all along, and maybe it was, it could very well have been. He rises up, your juices on his lips, chin, cheek, and he looks like he's been dining like an animal – or maybe on one.

Your breath comes back to you slowly, and both men are there, looking down, cocks still hard, waiting on your command.

You're too exhausted to do anything your self – but that doesn't mean you can't tell them to do things.

"Lay down," you command, and they both do so, as you rise up.

You lean in and kiss both of them, the darker man tasting of you, and the blonde tasting you second hand, and then you rock back onto your knees.

You take the dark man's hand and put it on the blonde's cock. The blonde gasps at this – and then you take his hand and put it on the darker man's balls. They look at you, realizing what you mean to let them do, hopeful and expectant.

"One – two -- three – go," you tell them, giving them permission to start. They start exploring one another's shafts slowly, not nervous but perhaps shy at being this exposed to you. You watch over them, feeling heat stir again, turned on by making them do what you want, even when you know it's what both of them want too. They take turns looking at you, but it's almost hotter when they don't, when their eyes are focused on each other, on their cocks, and hands – or when their eyes close because everything's beginning to feel so good for them. You can see them trying to match their pace, but it's hard when each of them is so hungry for what comes next. The blonde dives in to kiss the darker man hard, and then you lean in and he kisses you fiercely, as fierce as the darker man's stroking his cock, and the darker man bites your shoulder and moans and you trail your hands down both of their stomachs, feeling the muscles there tense, skin hitting skin so fast it's like the sound of rain.

The darker man gasps and thrusts forward into the blonde's hand, his hips taking off, and then the blonde's trying to wait but he can't, he cries out, his cock pummeling the darker man's hand. Cum squirts out of them just like your juices did from you, utterly unrestrained, landing on sheets and thighs.

Now everything's wet, and everyone is wet, sticky, and panting. You wish you could stay here forever – but while the night's still young, you know you should try other doors.

Pick up your clothing and turn to page 191.

ou reach between your own legs and underneath your skirt. Your underwear is still between your finger and your clit, but that doesn't matter – watching the men has made you so sensitive that you awaken at the slightest touch. On the bed they rock back and forth, hypnotically. The darker man's eyes are closed in pleasure, every inch of him being eaten by the blonde, and the blonde man comes up on him again and again – and then casts a furtive glance at you where he can see your legs open wide as your hand strokes between them.

He starts going faster, egging you on. You stroke yourself, using two fingers, rubbing hard, as he almost gags on the darker man's thick hard cock, speeding up. The darker man gives up on holding onto the poster and instead, puts his hands on the blonde's shoulders, then runs his fingers into his light hair, his exquisite ass clenching with each thrust. The blonde takes him deep and reaches up to stroke his balls and you press against yourself harder, faster, trying to keep their time, legs spread wide on the expensive chair you're in, your body acting like it's you up there getting fucked hard by the dark man, trying to let all of him in as you rub so very hard.

The darker man curls forward, and you can see the expression on his face as his need mounts him, the groans turning into gasps as his climax nears, the blonde sucking on him for all he's worth. Your own hips arc forward of their own accord, you as well turned into a wild beast of heat and need – and when the darker man cries out, hips thrusting desperately into the blonde's open mouth, you arc forward, ready, and touch yourself that one final time, the one that pushes you over the edge and into the abyss.

Waves of pleasure wrack through your body as you sink back into the chair. The darker man sags forward, spent, while the blonde rises up, as smug as a cat that's eaten a canary.

The wet strip on the fabric between your legs feels like it's a mile wide. And when he can breathe again, the darker man looks at you, his gaze predatory, a hand reaching down to stroke his cock. "Are you sure you don't want to join us?" he asks, and the blonde stretches his arm out.

If you'd like to join them, flip to page 196.

If you want to go back into the hall, turn to page 192.

*D*enying yourself is difficult and yet you feel it will later grant you greater rewards. The House is yours until dawn – there's no reason you can't watch now and play later. You've never seen two men like this before, in person, fucking just for you. It's like watching pornography.

And they know they're performing. Watching them rock back and forth is hypnotic. The darker man's eyes are closed in pleasure, every inch of him being eaten by the blonde, and the blonde man comes up on him again and again – and then casts a furtive glance at you. He wants you to see what he's capable of doing – what he could be doing for you. And the darker man, in between heavy breaths, turns to gives you the kind of looks that make you wonder what it would be like to be beneath him, to have him find his way inside you. It's easy to imagine his cock filling you up, instead of the blonde's mouth. And the blonde's cock is still hard, curled up towards his stomach, aching to be touched.

Together they build, the darker man's hands on the blonde's shoulders, then in his hair, as they speed up, moving as one, the darker man's ass clenching drum-tight with each thrust, making low grunts that seem to claim the blonde, until he cries out, and his whole body pulses in waves, chest, stomach, hips. The darker man thrusts helplessly into the blonde's willing mouth until he lets out a gasp and a final low moan, and the blonde rises up, lips wet, looking smug.

When the darker man is composed again, barely, he looks hungrily at the blonde. "Lay down," he says, and the blonde willingly obeys.

The show isn't over yet. You lean forward at the edge of your seat to see what – or who – will come next.

The darker man's cock is hard again somehow. He pushes the blonde's legs apart, and the blonde gasps, his untouched cock still hard against his stomach. The darker man puts one hand on the blonde's shoulders, and uses the other to guide his cock, still wet with spit and cum, in.

The blonde lets out a long low moan as the dark man's cock enters him. His hand finds his own cock and begins to stroke it as the dark man begins thrusting, sliding easily in and out of him. They kiss, and your lips part, imagining being there, being touched, getting fucked.

The dark man raises his head, looks over at you, and catches your wide-eyed stare.

"It's not too late for you to join," he says, his voice low.

Do keep watching? Turn to page 238.

Do you go towards the bed? Head to page 239.

ou shake your head. You're wet, but you don't want to interrupt this moment between the two of them.

"If you change your mind, Mistress, let us know," the dark man says.

But then his eyes aren't for you anymore, they're for the blonde man that he's arching over, all the muscles of his hips and thighs propelling him forward into the blonde's ass. The blonde grunts with each thrust, his hands torn between pulling the dark man's ass further into him, and stroking his own hard cock. He plays his hands up the dark man's back and kisses him again and then gasps as he's pinned anew. Slowly he can't help but touch himself more, as the dark man's thrusts become more intent. The dark man leans down and kisses him savagely, his mouth and then his throat, but then his hands find places on either side of the blonde man's shoulders and he starts to moan with each increasing thrust, his pleasure building inside of him.

The blonde man's stomach begins to tighten as his hands play faster on his cock, as he's filled by the darker man's cock again and again, skin sliding over skin, friction building hot, until the blonde man shudders convulsively and cum spills out in a silver arc onto his own pale stomach. The dark man fucks him through this with a groan and then his voice breaks into a shout as his hips buck forward madly, shooting out his own cum deep into the blonde's ass.

They collapse on the bed, panting for breath, but when they're done they look over to you.

Do you go back into the hall? If so, turn to page 191.

Or do you decide to join them? Go to page 239.

ou take off your clothing as you as you cross the room towards the bed. You've watched for long enough. Both men reach out an arm for you. Whose do you take first?

The blonde's? Turn to 240.

The darker man's? Flip to 242.

ou take the blonde's hand first. You're not sure where there's room for you between them, how you'll fit in, but you don't want to be left out anymore.

The blonde reaches up towards your face and catches his fingers in your hair. You let yourself be guided down to kiss him. His lips are strong and his tongue finds yours, his whole body moving gently beneath you as the dark man slowly starts fucking him again. He uses a fistful of your hair to pull your head back, breaking the kiss, his eyes focused only on you, although the dark man entering him again makes him groan.

Then the blonde reaches for your legs to pull you over – he meant what he said about you joining in. You carefully move to straddle him, facing the darker man, so that your pussy hovers far above the blonde's mouth – and it's the dark man's turn to pull you near.

You fall into him as he kisses you roughly, lip smashing against yours, a low growl in his throat, him still fucking the blonde beneath you. You get dizzy -- you're really here, in between them, kissing both of them – and when he releases you, you sink down, all self-consciousness lost – and find the blonde waiting for you with his tongue. He licks you and you gasp, startled, and try to rise up – but his hands catch at your waist and guide you back down to his tongue again. You settle in, openmouthed, as his tongue starts running over your pussy and clit, back to front, front to back. You hold onto the darker man's shoulders for support, kissing his chest and neck, as he continues to thrust, making all three of you rock in turn. His hands slide up your body, clutching at your breasts, pinching your nipples, just as the blonde's tongue starts to probe into you, pressing against your walls, chin rubbing against your clit, the long groans he's making as he's fucked getting muffled by your pussy.

Each of the darker man's thrusts are getting telegraphed into you, rocking the blonde's body, making him lose a second of concentration each time. You see the blonde's hard cock, curved up against his stomach, and you reach for it. When you touch it he entirely stops in surprise – and then starts eating you out desperately as you stroke it for him. His hands clutch at your thighs, pulling your hips down, so that his tongue can go further inside you. When it's out of you he sucks on your clit like it's a candy, running his tongue's tip over you again and again. You start to ride into his face, unable to help yourself, and completely unwilling to stop.

The dark man groans, as the blonde's ass keeps taking his cock, and he pulls his fingernails up your exposed back. You hold yourself up with one hand and keep pulling at the blonde's cock with the other, taking your hand from hilt to head and then back. His cock starts to twitch inside your hand like the living thing it is – and then he lets go of your thighs and plants a hand on either cheek of your ass.

Before you can question this change, the blonde has spread you wide and is pressing his tongue into your darkest place. You gasp, and he reaches one hand around to keep rubbing your clit while his tongue darts quickly in and out of you.

It is this last sensation that makes you lost. You suddenly tense and then cry out a wild sound, unprepared for the force of the orgasm that his tongue and hand have unleashed. The dark man speeds up and you manage to reach for the blonde's cock again to stroke it just in time to have him burst for you, white cum gushing out of his twitching head. You both are lost to your orgasms while the dark man quickly catches up, pounding the blonde's ass until he rams forward one final time with a long low groan that ends in a breathless gasp as he fills the blonde up with cum.

You collapse onto the bed and don't know how long you lay there, only that you have to, for a time, until the world stops spinning. But after that, you know it's time to go out to the hallway again.

Pick up your clothing and turn to 191.

he darker man's hand guides you up onto the bed. You're not sure how you can fit in, but you know you want to. The dark man gets a wicked look on his face, and tells you to, "Turn around."

You do as you're told, and the dark man pulls you gently over so that you're squatting over the blonde man's face, facing further up the bed. You feel like some sort of animal, but as he starts licking at you, you no longer mind. The dark man's hands stroke down your back, first gently, and then fingers-clawed, as the blonde's tongue laps from your pussy up to your clit. You moan a little and settle lower, giving the blonde's tongue more access, which he starts to use, sucking on your lips and on your clit, trying to bring you even closer down to him.

What you don't expect is the dark man's hands, stroking down your back and ass, and then him spreading your ass wide and slowing pushing one finger inside of your pussy. You shudder as he starts to finger you, and you're trapped, between the blonde's tongue on your clit and the friction of the dark man's finger – now two of them – exploring inside. He makes broad circles and then a come hither motion inside of you, stroking you inside with each of his strokes into the blonde, as you gasp and the blonde moans.

You no longer think about looking like an animal, as your knees spread even wider and your hips begin to ride the blonde's tongue. He's bobbing under you with each stroke that pins his ass and his breath is hot against your pussy and the inside of your thighs. The dark man slides a third finger into you, and you feel yourself stretch around him, your pussy welcoming him in. He starts to fuck you with his hand now, faster than he's fucking the blonde, and you feel wide and ever so willing. You grab hold of the sheets for balance, the key pressed under your hand, as you're pinned over the blonde's tongue. The blonde's losing control, it's all he can do to keep his mouth open and tongue out so that you can ride over it.

Then the dark man stops and both of you groan, feeling lost. He pulls his hand out of you and you wonder what you did wrong – and if you can demand that he start up again – when another finger is pressed inside of you, and then removed and placed against your own ass. You tense as, wet with juices from yourself, the dark man presses his thumb in, and takes another stroke. The blonde groans just as you do. You're completely exposed to him, to both of them -- and you like it. The darker man leaves his thumb inside you then carefully pushes his other fingers back into your pussy and starts making circles with his whole hand, stretching you out in all directions, as the blonde begins desperately licking your clit again. The feeling is intense, and you slow down to just this one moment, being pressed, pulled, and filled, and the dark man starts rocking his hand back and forth, taking your ass and your pussy in turns, as he starts to fuck you as he's fucking the blonde. There's nothing you can do, everything feels too good, and you're not in control of anything about this, nor do you want to be. Your knees slide wider, the blonde's tongue is frantic against your clit and the dark man's hand is relentless as he fucks you both.

Sheets wind in your hands and you cry out into the mattress as your orgasm rockets through you, ass and pussy grasping at his hand. The dark man responds, pressing harder into you until your hip's final shudder and he relents. He pulls his hand out, and your body can still feel the space it created inside. You sink forward, spent, and then curl around to watch the blonde get fucked.

You realize how much the blonde was denying himself to help you get off, his hard cock laying against his stomach, ignored. He reaches for it, but you stop him.

"Please, Mistress," he says, giving you an anguished look, your juices still covering his chin.

You crawl closer on the bed, pinning down his nearest arm with your body. The dark man watches you, still sliding in and out, balls deep into the blonde's ass.

You rise up. The blonde made you happy, didn't he? Perhaps happiness deserves to be rewarded. You lean out and put your mouth on the head of his cock, and he whispers, "Oh God."

You sink your mouth down around him as he lets out a ragged

gasp. The dark man thrusts again, and you match him in time, so that you're both working over the blonde. You take his smooth cock into the back of your throat again and again, lips tight around his shaft. The blonde's hand runs up and into your hair, pulling and pushing, and below you his hips start to shake. The dark man's thrusts become more wild as he begins to lose control, and the blonde whispers, "Mistress, mistress –" in warning as you feel his cock become arrow straight inside your mouth, then gush out with hot cum. The darker man gives three final thrusts, each one harder than the last, until he shouts aloud and fills the blonde's ass with his load.

You swallow everything and rise up, looking down at the plain adoration of the blonde. "Thank you, so much."

"Of course," you say, as though you do this sort of thing often. You grin at the both of them, and then make your way off the bed. Picking up your clothing, you head out to the hall.

Turn to 191.

a house ready and waiting to serve you. Who has ever heard of such a thing? It sounds like the plot to a horror film. You throw the box with its fine linen note in the trash, but for a time keep the key on a chain around your neck. It is pretty, after all.

THE END — but you can turn to page 249.

If you would like to return to the beginning, flip back to the first page.

ou look into the car, at the sweeping leather upholstery and swank electronics, and you get scared. You've never been in any car this nice before – and you're too worried about how you will fit in, wherever it is that it will go when it leaves. Your fear makes you hesitant and in that moment, all bravery is lost. You step back, and the woman looks at you, waiting. She is as beautiful and exotic as the car is, which makes you feel even more out of place.

Holding the key hot in your hand, you run back into the terminal for the plane.

You tell yourself later that you made the right decision but on rare moments when you're honest with yourself you're never really sure.

Turn to page 249 if you're through.

If you would like to return to the beginning, go back to page one.

"ake me back to the airport, please."

A frown creases the woman's perfect brow. "Are you sure?" Her concern feels genuine.

You swallow and nod, looking at the immense structure behind her. You have felt small in your life many times before. This is yet another chance.

"He chose you for a reason. You're meant to be here," she says encouragingly.

"Why?" you ask her, because *he* is not around.

She breaks into a guilty smile, ducking her head a little as though you've caught her. "I don't know. But you can ask him yourself, if you stay."

"What's the point of all –" you begin, but she shakes her head.

"I'm sorry, but I've told you all I can. The rest is up to you. It's always up to you." She makes the door sway, the implication obvious – stay, or go.

Do you exit the car? If so, turn to page 6.

If you return to the airport, turn to page 248.

She drives you back to the airport in silence, and you feel as though you're watching a film backwards, or going on a rollercoaster the wrong way. The hills reverse and the road fattens until the city is on the horizon, and traffic finds the car again. It is evening and the airport is quiet this time of day, it is easy for her to park beside the curb.

You want to ask her if you've made the right choice, but you don't think she'd answer you, or that you'd like her answer if she did. So she opens the door for you and you slink out with just a nod. As the door closes behind you, you get the same feeling that you've had before, of opportunity being lost, and watching the car drive off you wonder how you let it slip through your fingers, again.

Flip to 249 if you're through.

If you would like to return to the beginning, turn back to the first page.

*T*hanks for reaching one of the many endings of The House! You all have no idea how fun doing this project was for me – it turns out I secretly like writing in second-person, who knew! I'd love to write more in this series, so if you enjoyed this, make sure to leave a review and let me know — they're kind of a pain to code on the back-end, but if there's interest, I'll go for it!

Keep reading for a sneak peek at Blood of the Pack, the first book in my Dark Ink Tattoo series, a sultry, sizzling dark paranormal set in Vegas!

For more about my other book, playlists, and cat photos, sign up for my mailing list by clicking on the word HERE or go to http://www.cassiealexander.com/newsletter.

BLOOD OF THE PACK: Dark Ink Tattoo Book One
Cassie Alexander

I HEARD an engine turn the corner, startled, and the MMA fighter I was touching up a truly regrettable tribal tattoo on yelped.

"Sorry. Spine," I apologized, peeking over his hulking shoulder to see Jack Stone arrive on time for work, possibly for the first time ever while in my employ. His black 1963 Lincoln Continental swooped through Dark Ink's parking lot like a hearse.

Just Jack. I knew what his car sounded like. Even though our shifts didn't overlap often – I'd heard it often enough to know it wasn't a bike. And still….

I sprayed my client's shoulder with cool water and wiped the blood away, trying to ignore the slight jitter in my hand. This was my job – this was my tattoo-shop – and I'd been doing tats for the past seven years in peace. I breathed deep and willed myself calm. I wasn't scared and I hadn't lost control, and if I kept telling myself that long enough eventually I might believe it.

I put the heel of my hand on the fighter's back to steady it and stepped on the pedal to get the gun roaring again, starting where I'd left off, cleaning up some cheaper artist's shoddy job. In no other profession was the phrase 'you get what you pay for' so true.

This time, the fighter twitched, not me. No way not to hit nerves when you were tattooing someone over bone. Tattoos on top of bone felt like you were getting stabbed.

A lot like getting menacing letters from your ex in prison.

FIVE MINUTES LATER, Jack was leaning over from the wrong side of the counter, purring my name. "Angela."

I didn't turn around. I knew where he was, of course, I'd just made it a habit to ignore him. Mostly.

"Hey, boss-lady, I'm on time, just like you asked," he tried again. I snorted, stopped working, and looked up.

A gaggle of barely-old-enough-to-be-in-the-shop girls flocked behind him, flipping through flash displays, clearly whispering to themselves about him. He was stare-worthy. If you were into tall, lean but muscular men, black hair, brown eyes, and full sleeve tattoos, Jack was your kind of guy. When our shifts overlapped I had to remind myself he was off limits the same way that ex-smokers have to remind themselves to forget about cigarettes. I knew it was for my own good – I'd quit men that were bad for me a long time ago – but that didn't make it any less hard.

It was also why I tried to ignore him. It was good for him sometimes.

"On time for once," I corrected him.

"It's winter," he said, like that was an explanation.

I saw the post office truck pull into the parking lot behind him and my stomach clenched. "Yeah, of course," I said without thinking, standing and pulling my gloves off. "Wrap him up, will you?" I said, sidling towards the hip-high swinging saloon door that divided our half of the shop from the client's.

"My pleasure," Jack said, setting his ass down on the piercing display case and spinning his legs over to switch sides. Normally I'd yell at him about that, but – I reached the door just as the postman did, opening it up to take our letters from him.

Junk mail, tattoo convention flyers, the electricity bill and – something stamped 'Approved by the LVMPD'.

Goddammit.

I bit my lips and ran for the office. I stopped myself from slamming the door, just barely, instead whirling to place my back against it, like that would help keep all the monsters at bay, and slowly sank to the floor.

I threw the rest of the mail to the ground and opened up Gray's letter.

Visit me.

Funny how it only took two words to blow my life apart. I bit the side of my hand to stop from screaming – but somewhere on the inside, a hidden part of me howled.

I tore his letter up – same as I'd torn the other three I'd gotten, starting two weeks ago, and threw the pieces of it into the trash. If only escaping Gray were so easy. I should've left years ago – given myself and Rabbit a head start – but then what? Keep running forever? When I knew Gray and the Pack would always be able to find us? No, instead I'd pretended that I'd had a normal life – that I was normal. I'd rolled the dice, praying that someone meaner and nastier than Gray would take him out in prison.

I should've known that no such person existed.

I'd lived in Vegas my whole life – you'd think by now I'd be a better gambler.

There was a quiet knock on the door behind me. "Boss-lady?" Jack's voice, full of concern.

I stood and straightened myself out, opening the door a crack. "I, uh, didn't know what to charge him – so I asked for two-fifty. That enough?" Jack asked.

It was way more than I'd have asked for. It was only a touch up, hadn't even taken an hour. "He paid that?"

"I can be very convincing," he said, and shrugged, searching what he could see of me with his expressive eyes.

"Stop that. If I wanted to tell you about it, I would."

He leaned forward and pressed the door open. I could've fought back – could've closed the door – but I didn't want to make a scene. But my office was meant for only one person, one desk, one chair, there was no way for us be in here and not be in one another's space. In other circumstances I'd thought about doing things to Jack in here that'd make even the most jaded local blush, but now – I'd much rather he hold me and lie to me that everything was going to be all right.

"What was that?" he said, jerking his chin at the other mail still littering the floor.

"Nothing."

He stared me down. Could he really read me? Or was he just one of those guys who made you think they could? The kind you had relationships with where you filled all the silences with too much hope?

"Seriously, Ang," he said, his voice low.

I gestured to include the entire parlor. "It all says it's for me."

"Even the one from the Las Vegas Metropolitan police department?" he asked. "Don't ask me how I know what stamped mail from prison looks like."

Damn, Jack being Jack. Too smart for his own good. "It's none of your business," I said, as boss-like as I could, shutting down the conversation.

Jack took his cue. "All right, all right,"

"And I need to go."

"Yeah, to your date, I know."

I hadn't told him I was going on a date tonight, that that was why I needed him to really-I-mean-it be on time for once. And he'd said it with almost precisely flat inflection, so I couldn't really tell if he was jealous or whatever – and it didn't matter, because I was with Mark now, anyhow. But some deep and secret part of me bared its teeth and wagged its tail.

He glanced down at the letters. "If anything bad comes of that, you let me know, okay?"

"Sure," I lied, and pushed past him, out the door.

Keep reading Blood of the Pack: Dark Ink Tattoo Book One – and just in case you missed the chance the first time, if you'd like to join Cassie's mailing list, click here or go to http://www.cassiealexander. com/newsletter – to find out about more books and secret scenes.

Written with Kara Lockharte (and possibly as our co-author name, Cassie Lockharte):
The Prince of the Otherworlds Series—sexy urban fantasy
Dragon Called
Dragon Destined
Dragon Fated
Dragon Mated
The Wardens of the Otherworlds Series—sexy urban fantasy
Dragon's Captive
Wolf's Princess
Wolf's Rogue
Dragon's Flame
Written as Cassie Alexander:
The Dark Ink Tattoo series—hot paranormal romance
Blood of the Pack: Dark Ink Tattoo Book One
Blood at Dusk: Dark Ink Tattoo Book Two
Blood by Moonlight: Dark Ink Tattoo Book Three
Blood by Midnight: Dark Ink Tattoo Book Four
Blood at Dawn: Dark Ink Tattoo Book Five
The Edie Spence urban fantasy series
Nightshifted
Moonshifted
Shapeshifted

<u>Deadshifted</u>

<u>Bloodshifted</u>

The House—a find your fantasy erotica

<u>The House</u>

Her Future Vampire Lover—futuristic vampire paranormal romance

<u>Her Future Vampire Lover</u>

Her Ex-boyfriend's Werewolf Lover—a sexy paranormal romance

<u>Her Ex-boyfriend's Werewolf Lover</u>

Rough Ghost Lover—a sizzling erotic horror—DOES NOT HAVE HEA

<u>Rough Ghost Lover</u>

www.ingramcontent.com/pod-product-compliance
Lightning Source LLC
Chambersburg PA
CBHW071246190726
48292CB00007B/2428